India wasn't going to argue with that. Halfway back
the first fat raindrops began to fall. She picked up
her pace, but when she looked over her shoulder
at the approaching storm she managed to twist her
ankle and break the heel of one of her blue-and-
white Mary Janes.

Liam was at her side almost quicker than she could
steady herself on her other foot. "Are you okay?"

"Yeah, I think so." She lifted her leg out to the side
to check out the damage. "More than I can say for
my poor shoe, though."

"At least you didn't break your ankle. It's just a shoe."

The rainfall upped its tempo a bit, and Liam let out
a long sigh. Before she could ask what was wrong,
her feet flew out from under her as Liam scooped
her up in his arms and started walking toward his
truck like some knight in shining armor.

Or cowboy in a tan Stetson.

Dear Reader,

Welcome back to Blue Falls, Texas, home to rolling hills full of vibrant wildflowers, that special small-town flavor and some smoking-hot cowboys. I loved writing about Blue Falls so much in my Teagues of Texas trilogy that I couldn't bear to leave it behind. So we all get to return to that slice of the Texas Hill Country in three new stories, the Blue Falls, Texas trilogy. These stories center around three women who have been best friends since their days at Blue Falls High School. Now they're all successful local businesswomen who, unbeknownst to them, have some hunky cowboy heroes in their futures.

Her Perfect Cowboy is the story of India Pike, who owns the local vintage-inspired clothing boutique, and Liam Parrish, a bronc rider and single dad who comes to town to organize the new series of benefit rodeos. I love opposites-attract romances, and that's exactly what India and Liam find themselves navigating. After all, what could a classy boutique owner and a rough-around-the-edges cowboy possibly have in common? It turns out that it's more than either of them would have guessed at their first meeting.

I hope you enjoy *Her Perfect Cowboy* and, in the months ahead, the stories of India's two best friends, Skyler Harrington and Elissa Mason, and their own perfect-for-them cowboys.

Trish Milburn

Her Perfect Cowboy

TRISH MILBURN

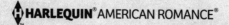

HARLEQUIN® AMERICAN ROMANCE®

Recycling programs
for this product may
not exist in your area.

ISBN-13: 978-0-373-75454-0

HER PERFECT COWBOY

Copyright © 2013 by Trish Milburn

This edition published by arrangement with Harlequin Books S.A.

For questions and comments about the quality of this book, please contact us at CustomerService@Harlequin.com.

® and ™ are trademarks of Harlequin Enterprises Limited or its corporate affiliates. Trademarks indicated with ® are registered in the United States Patent and Trademark Office, the Canadian Trade Marks Office and in other countries.

Printed in U.S.A.

Ⓗ **HARLEQUIN**®
™ www.Harlequin.com

ABOUT THE AUTHOR

Trish Milburn writes contemporary romance for Harlequin American Romance, paranormal romance for Harlequin Nocturne and self-publishes some of her other titles. She's a two-time Golden Heart award winner, a fan of walks in the woods and road trips, and is a big geek girl, including being a dedicated Whovian and Browncoat. She loves *Doctor Who* so much that she dressed up as the Tenth Doctor for Dragon*Con last year, complete with her very own sonic screwdriver, and plans to have an Eleventh Doctor costume for the con this year.

Books by Trish Milburn

HARLEQUIN AMERICAN ROMANCE

*The Teagues of Texas

To Michelle Butler for introducing me to the Texas Hill Country, and to Mary Fechter for always being willing to hit the road to the Hill Country with me when I come visit.

Chapter One

India Pike folded back the tissue paper at the top of the box and pulled out the floor-length dress, its red-and-white vertical stripes and the swirling piping on the bodice harkening back to the 1940s.

"That's gorgeous." Elissa Mason grasped the sides of the long skirt and spread it wide. "Makes me feel like I've been transported back in time."

"Good, since that's what I'm going for." India waved her hand to indicate the racks of vintage-inspired clothing around them.

The front door of Yesterwear Boutique opened to reveal the final member of their trio, Skyler Harrington. "Sorry I'm late. We had a bit of an emergency at the inn this morning. Hot water heater decided it was time for a vacation." Skyler probably hadn't spent more than a couple of minutes outside, but the heat of the Texas sun had already caused her fair complexion to flush. That and her tendency to always be on the go, a bit like a redheaded tornado.

India glanced at the clock on the wall. "You're not late."

"Most people call this on time," Elissa said.

Skyler ignored their familiar teasing and placed her leather-bound notebook on the glass-top counter that housed the boutique's collection of faux vintage jewelry. "I jotted down some ideas for our next BlueBelles class."

"I'm shocked, I tell you, shocked," India said as she made her way to the round table in the corner. The carved daisies on the top of the table showed an attention to detail—one of the reasons Ryan Teague's custom furniture was so in demand. She poured her friends cold glasses of lemonade.

"You two act like there's something wrong with being organized," Skyler said.

Elissa wrapped her arm around Skyler and guided her toward the table. "Not at all. We love you just how you are."

Skyler rolled her eyes and took her seat so they could get to work on planning the program for their next girls' enrichment class.

Even though the BlueBelles classes had been India's idea, they were a labor of love for all of them. The planning and execution that went into the classes never felt like work. The three of them had been fortunate to find success in their separate businesses, so they used that success whenever they could to give back to the community. The BlueBelles classes were their way of showing young girls that they could succeed just as the three of them had.

"What do you have?" India asked Skyler, willing to wait on her own ideas until her friends had shared theirs.

"Money management, organizational skills, maybe a tour of the inn to see how to run a hospitality business," Skyler said, reading from her list.

"Good ideas, but maybe we can pair one of those with something a little lighter and fun," India said. "What do you have, Elissa?"

"I have a friend in Dallas who is a therapist. Maybe something about self-esteem. Or since it's spring, we could focus on native plant gardening."

India consulted her own ideas but didn't speak.

"I know that look," Skyler said. "What are you thinking?"

"We always have more ideas than we can use. What if instead of our normal single class we have several in an all-day conference? We could offer a wider variety."

"Oh, I like that idea," Elissa said.

Skyler thought for a moment then nodded, too.

As they dived into the particulars, the front door opened again.

Verona Charles, Elissa's aunt, walked in with a wave. "Hey, girls. I'm so glad I caught you all here together."

"Oh, that can't be good," Elissa quipped, earning her a playful swat on the shoulder from Verona.

"Ignore her and have a seat," India said. She reached toward the fresh pitcher of lemonade in the middle of the table. "Would you like a drink?"

"That would be lovely. Can't believe how hot it is already." Verona smoothed her short, gently curling silver hair.

"It's Texas, and you've lived here all your life," Elissa said as India poured another glass of lemonade.

"I know. Guess I'm just getting too old for the heat."

Elissa snorted. "If you're getting old, I'm a green troll."

At five foot ten, trim and tanned with long, deep brown hair, Elissa was as far from a green troll as a girl could get.

"Lippy, I tell you," Verona said. "Lippy just like your mother."

Elissa smiled wide, causing Verona to roll her eyes and shift her attention away from her niece. Her actions and words fooled no one. She adored the ground her niece walked on. Elissa was like the child Verona never had, and she was nothing less than a second mother to Elissa.

"You have that look," Skyler said. "The one that says you have a grand plan in play."

"I don't have a plan yet, but that's something I thought you three could help me with." Verona took a sip of her lemonade. "I was just over at the tourism office, and Blake said they are looking for something new to draw in more tourists, something to keep the numbers up once the bluebonnets fade away."

"Let me guess," India said. "You volunteered to help think of something."

"What can I say? Retirement is boring." Verona scooted forward in her chair a little bit. "I went by the bakery afterward to pick up some fresh bread, and Keri told me that Jake Monroe's little girl, Mia, is about to start her cancer treatments."

"Poor little girl," India murmured.

"That's when it hit me," Verona said. "We can accomplish two goals with one event—come up with something that would bring in tourists but have it be a benefit for Mia."

"Oh, that is a good idea," Skyler said. "I'd be happy to help with something like that."

Verona patted Skyler's hand atop the table. "Thank you, dear." She made eye contact with Elissa then India. "Can I count on both of you to help out, too?"

"Can't say no to that," Elissa said.

India considered the workload of planning the Blue-Belles classes as well as the community event, but then she had one of those lightbulb moments like Verona had at the Mehlerhaus Bakery. "We were just talking about expanding the next BlueBelles offering to several classes. We could have a day-long conference the same day as this community event and donate all the proceeds to Mia's medical expenses." Skyler and Elissa quickly nodded their agreement.

"That's a wonderful offer," Verona said, her voice growing more excited. "Okay, then, I guess we just need to figure out what type of event would bring a lot of people to town and be of interest to the locals, too."

Over the next several minutes, they tossed out any idea

that popped into their heads—an arts-and-crafts show, a play, a singing competition. While they all held merit, none really popped and said, "Hey, I'll make a ton of money!"

India rubbed her eyes then glanced out the window just as a truck pulling a horse trailer drove down Main Street. "What about a rodeo? What could be more Texas than that?"

Elissa leaned forward. "Perfect. And bonus, hot cowboys in town."

"Gone through all the single men in the county already?" Skyler asked.

"Hey, that makes me sound bad. What's wrong with going out for drinks or dancing, having a good time?"

"Nothing, dear," Verona said. "But maybe it's time to pick one of these young men to settle down with."

Elissa leaned back in her chair and pointed at her aunt. "Oh, no. You can just direct your matchmaking juju in another direction."

After the laughter died down, Skyler flipped to a new page on her notepad and started taking notes as they all offered up ideas and a to-do list.

"Now we need to divide these up," Skyler said after her legal pad was full of bulleted action items.

"I'll be the liaison with the tourism bureau," Verona said. "Since this was your brainchild, India, it makes sense for you to take point on contacting rodeo companies to see about scheduling."

"Me? I don't know the first thing about rodeo."

Elissa leaned forward. "Hot guys in tight jeans. That's all you need to know."

"Then you do it."

"Nope. I'll head up the planning for the BlueBelles conference and round up some sponsors for things like advertising."

India shifted her gaze to Skyler. "You grew up on a ranch."

"And haven't lived there in years on purpose. Besides, I'll work on the food vendors and the barbecue cook-off. The rodeo is all yours."

India sighed but didn't see any way to wiggle out of this one. When she heard her father's voice in her memory telling her she'd bitten off more than she could chew, she shook her head. She might not be a rodeo expert, but she was reasonably intelligent. She could do this, and no remembered taunts by her useless father were going to tell her otherwise.

"It'll be good for you," Elissa said. "You need to get out of this shop more. And if you find a little hot cowboy lovin', so much the better."

India eyed her friend. "Seriously, can you imagine me with some rough-around-the-edges cowboy?"

Elissa waggled her eyebrows. "Honey, I can imagine anyone with a smokin' hot cowboy."

Ten minutes after her friends left, India was still sitting at the table kicking herself for opening her mouth. This was going to be the worst rodeo ever.

LIAM PARRISH DROVE down the hill into the small town of Blue Falls. It'd been a few years since he'd driven through this part of the Hill Country, but it was still as pretty as he remembered. It was well past bluebonnet season, but this area of Texas still looked like a different world entirely from the urban environment of Fort Worth or the starkness of his West Texas hometown. Instead of vast expanses of flat, flat, flat, the Hill Country was home to more landscape variety—rugged limestone and granite hills, groupings of prickly pear cactus, caves and spring-fed rivers. One minute you might be passing a winery, the next a local watering hole that looked as if it'd been in business since Texas became a state.

When he reached Main Street in Blue Falls, he started looking for his destination. He spotted a restaurant called the Primrose Café, an antique store, the Frothy Stein bar, a bakery and an old-time hardware store. His eyes caught the name of Yesterwear Boutique, the clothing store where he was supposed to meet India Pike.

All the parking spaces along Main seemed to be full, a good sign that the town wasn't dying and thus unable to support a rodeo. He found a spot to park his truck on a side street then walked back to the shop. The moment he stepped inside the cool interior, his nose twitched at the smell of some flowery scent. And then he took in his surroundings, which looked like a sea of feminine froufrou. Dresses, hats, shoes, jewelry. Was that a petticoat on the headless mannequin in the corner?

It was official. He'd never felt more out of place in his life.

He shifted from one foot to the other and tipped back his hat just in time to see a woman come through the doorway that led to another room full of clothes. A beautiful woman with wavy black hair that rested lightly on her shoulders. When she saw him, her eyes widened enough that he thought they were a grayish-blue. She recovered quickly and stepped fully into the entry area that held the cash register, a display counter full of jewelry and little beaded purses, and a few items of clothing.

"Mr. Parrish?"

"Yes, ma'am. Sorry I'm a bit late. There was an accident about an hour north of here."

"No problem." After what seemed like a moment of hesitation, she took a couple of steps toward him and extended her hand. "India Pike. I appreciate you driving all the way to Blue Falls."

The moment his hand wrapped around hers to shake, he realized how tiny her hand was, completely disappearing in his. The handshake was brief, but it was long enough for him to label her as delicate.

"It was a nice day to get out of the city and go for a drive." He laughed. "You'd think as much time as I spend on the road that the driving would get old, but there's something about the open road that's relaxing."

Well, wasn't he chatty all of a sudden?

He mentally shook himself and gestured over his shoulder. "I saw the café down the street looked busy. Must mean they have good food. Have you eaten?"

"Yes, actually. But if you'd like to go have lunch, we can meet sometime this afternoon."

Was it his imagination or did she seem less than excited about this meeting? Was she preoccupied? In a bad mood? Or maybe she just didn't have a clue what she was doing. He was used to meeting with fellow cowboys or middle-aged businessmen, not a dark-haired beauty wearing a dark blue dress and blue-and-white shoes.

"Nah, I can wait." Time to stop stealing glances at her legs and get down to business. "Best thing to do first is look at your facilities to see if they're suitable for a good-size rodeo, and what adjustments may need to be made."

She nodded. "Let me just lock up."

He stepped out onto the sidewalk, able to breathe deeper once he was out of the shop and farther from the woman who ran it. While he waited for her to flip over her sign saying she'd be back in thirty minutes and lock the door, he ran his hand over his face.

When was the last time he'd gotten an immediate jolt when he first laid eyes on a woman? Oh, yeah, Charlotte.

That certainly cooled his interest. He glanced at India Pike in her stylish getup that had a hint of some other era and realized she was a fancy woman, concerned with appearances just like Charlotte had been. A woman didn't dress and apply her makeup with such care if she wasn't concerned with what other people thought about her.

"Mr. Parrish?"

Damn it, he'd been staring and somehow managed to miss the obvious fact that India had turned toward him.

"Yeah. My truck is just around the corner."

"I'm parked out back. I'll get my car, and you can follow me."

"Okay." But when they reached the end of the alley that ran behind the line of shops, it was blocked by a delivery truck. "You can ride with me. I'm parked right here." He pointed toward his pickup, two spaces down from where they stood.

India looked back at the delivery truck again before agreeing.

When they reached his vehicle, he opened the door for her. She hesitated again before placing her hand in his so he could help her up. Her fingers felt so small and soft in his, and he caught a whiff of the same flowery scent he had in the store. He didn't know why, but it made him think of pale pink rose petals, the kind that were silky when you ran your fingers across them.

"Thank you," she said when she was seated.

He reluctantly let go of her hand, shut the door then spent the time it took him to walk around to the driver's side telling himself to snap out of it. Instant infatuations never led to anything good. Best to let them pass without acting on them. When he slid into his seat, he sensed more than saw how tense she was. Maybe she was just anxious about getting into a vehicle with someone she didn't know.

"We can wait until the alley is clear if you want," he said, waving a hand toward where two guys were unloading a grandfather clock behind the antique store.

"No, it's okay. The fairgrounds aren't far." She pointed out the windshield. "Go down a block and turn left."

He followed her directions for all of three minutes before they arrived at the fairgrounds, where he could see an arena, a grandstand, stables and a couple of smaller outbuildings. Small, but workable. He hurried out of the truck and went around to open her door. Just before he touched her dainty hand, he started reciting state capitals in his head. Once India was on solid ground, he released her and started walking toward the arena.

"You said on the phone that this would be a benefit rodeo," he said.

"Yes, for a little girl who is undergoing cancer treatments."

His heart squeezed. "How old is she?"

"Eight."

"Same age as my daughter." He couldn't imagine Ginny having to fight for her life like that, not when she should be playing and enjoying each new experience to the fullest. He looked toward India in time to notice her eyeing his hand, searching for a ring. He lifted his left hand and wiggled his bare fingers. "Ginny's mother and I aren't together." Now why had he felt the need to offer up that nugget of information?

"I'm sorry," she said, sounding embarrassed.

"I'm not." Shifting focus, he pointed toward the arena. "You've got a good basic setup here, but we'll have to make some adjustments."

"Whatever you think we need, as long as it's not too expensive."

He glanced toward India again, noticing she was shading her eyes against the sun. "You need a hat." He thumped the front edge of his.

"I'm not much of a cowgirl," she said. "Like at all. I can't even ride a horse."

"You're not from here?"

"I grew up here. Just…didn't have much opportunity to learn. And animals and I don't get along too well."

Just as he thought, one-hundred-percent girly female. How could you live in Texas your entire life and not learn how to ride a horse? He tried to picture her on one, but it only resulted in a ridiculous image in his head.

"Have you had rodeos here before?"

"Small ones, mainly roping events. Blue Falls is known more for wildflower tours and shopping."

Things more in her comfort zone.

"If you don't mind me asking, why are you the one heading this up?"

She looked up at him, dropping her hand when a dark cloud covered the sun. "That obvious that I'm ill-placed, huh?"

"A little." He smiled at her heavy sigh and quirk of her lips. Really nicely shaped lips.

"Let's say I got roped into it before I knew quite what happened."

He laughed as he leaned his arms against the top rail of the arena's fence. "I think we've all been there at one point or another."

As they discussed a few more details, he had to keep his eyes averted. If he didn't, they kept straying to her lips, making him wonder if they were as soft as they looked. Damn it, he needed to stop hanging out with cowboys or eight-year-olds all the time and go on an actual date. And not with someone who wouldn't know a steer from a dairy cow. He'd been down the fancy-girl route before, and it hadn't ended well. The only good thing he could say about his time with Charlotte was that he got the best kid in the world out of the deal. Ginny was worth the punches he'd taken to his heart. But he wasn't about to invite another round.

AS SHE LISTENED TO THUNDER in the distance, India discovered it was much easier to talk to Liam Parrish if he wasn't looking at her. For someone who was used to looking people in the eye all day, trying to connect with them so they'd feel comfortable in her store, how she felt around him was new. And it wasn't just because he was a guy. She wasn't one of those women who went all giggly and shy around men. Some of her good friends were guys. But there was something about this man in particular that was making her jumpy.

Like how he's a tall, sexy cowboy? She heard the words in her mind in Elissa's teasing voice. India was going to kill her friend for putting those kinds of thoughts in her head, making it difficult to conduct simple business. And then she was going to go after Verona for getting her into this mess in the first place. Her place was back in the shop, not out here where she halfway felt as if she were speaking a foreign language. And she'd taken French and Spanish, not Rodeo-ese, when she was a student at Blue Falls High School.

She was so caught up fantasizing about her plans for revenge that she missed part of what Liam said. "I'm sorry, what?"

He looked at her then, making her want to squirm with the intensity of his gaze. She couldn't tell the color of his eyes, shaded as they were by the brim of his hat, but she had the oddest sensation they were green. And she loved green eyes. Most of his hair was covered by the hat, but she could tell it was trimmed short and a golden brown.

"I know you're doing this as a benefit," he said, obviously for the second time. "But in order to get the type of competitors who will draw the kind of crowd you want, you'll have to offer good prize money."

"Oh, okay. How much?"

He quoted her a figure and thankfully shifted his attention away again.

"I'll have to ask what the budget is for this," she said. "We're planning some other activities to coincide with the rodeo, so I need to get with the people planning those and figure out the numbers."

He nodded.

A loud clap of thunder startled India so much that she yelped.

Liam looked up at the sky. "The storm is moving fast. We better get back to the truck."

She wasn't going to argue with that. Halfway back to his truck, the first fat raindrops began to fall. She picked up her pace, but when she looked back over her shoulder at the approaching storm she managed to twist her ankle and break the heel of one of her blue-and-white Mary Janes.

Liam was at her side almost quicker than she could steady herself on her other foot. "Are you okay?"

"Yeah, I think so." She lifted her leg out to the side to check out the damage. "More than I can say for my poor shoe, though."

"At least you didn't break your ankle. It's just a shoe."

"A shoe that cost me a hundred dollars," she mumbled under her breath.

Something changed in the air, and it had nothing to do with the storm. When she met Liam's eyes, his expression had hardened. Gone was the hint of laughter and open friendliness, replaced by tight lines and a distance that hadn't been there before.

The rainfall upped its tempo a bit, and Liam let out a long sigh. Before she could ask what was wrong, her feet flew out from under her as he scooped her up in his arms and started walking toward his truck like some knight in shining armor.

Or cowboy in a tan Stetson.

Chapter Two

India's skin blazed so hot that she was surprised Liam didn't drop her. But he didn't seem to notice her out-of-control embarrassment and maintained his strong hold on her as if she weighed next to nothing. Despite the rain, his feet never slipped. The short distance to his truck seemed to take aeons to cross, and yet at the same time a part of her felt it was over much too soon when he set her on her feet. She didn't even have time to take a breath before he pulled open the passenger door so she could escape the rain.

She scrambled inside just as the sky truly opened up. Liam had to be soaked before he even reached the front of the truck. He was nothing more than a vague blur as she watched him through the torrents of rain. By the time he dived into the driver's seat, he looked as if he'd taken a plunge in the lake. India's gaze traveled to where his blue button-up shirt was plastered to his chest and his jeans molded to what looked like a pair of powerful thighs.

Liam pulled off his drenched Stetson and tossed it onto the seat between them. As it landed, his gaze met hers and held for what had to be the longest second in human history.

She jerked her gaze away before she had time to think about what that might reveal—that she'd been ogling the mighty fine contours of his body.

"Been a while since I've seen a rain this hard," Liam said.

Thankful for something to think about other than what Liam Parrish hid beneath his plastered-to-his-skin clothing, India forced herself to focus on the rain hammering against the truck's windshield. Drought had become a dusty way of life in Texas lately, so they sorely needed the rain. Still, she would have been a lot happier if it had waited until they'd gotten back to her store. There, she wouldn't have to be trapped in a confined area with a man who seemed to fill most of the space available.

She leaned forward. "This keeps up and the arena will become a pool, and we'll have to switch from a rodeo to swimming races."

Liam laughed a little, and that unexpected response allowed India to take her first full breath since he'd picked her up. She ventured a quick glance at him and noticed the tightness in his expression from before had faded. She didn't know why it mattered so much to her, but she experienced a great sense of relief. She didn't like people being angry with her, and for some reason Liam Parrish had been, if only for a few brief moments.

The rain continued to pour down as if trying to make up for a year's worth of drought in one afternoon, and India searched desperately for something to talk about. They'd already covered all the particulars of the site, at least until she could touch base with Verona and Blake at the tourism bureau. His job, that was it. Men loved talking about their jobs, right?

"So, have you been running a rodeo company for long?" She kept her eyes averted, afraid they would return to those tantalizing muscles.

"Just a couple of years. I was riding the circuit before that. Still ride some when I get to missing it too much."

"Bulls?" Even she knew that was the event all the adrenaline-junkie cowboys liked.

"Broncs. I'm not crazy enough to get on a bull."

This time, it was her turn to laugh. "A smart man. Well, at least somewhat. Not sure how wise it is to get on any animal whose sole goal is to buck you off its back."

"You might be right about that, but the world's got to have at least a few crazy people to keep things interesting."

From her brief time with Liam Parrish, she could safely say he could keep things interesting without ever going anywhere near an animal.

She clamped a mental lid on her thoughts. Damn, was this rain ever going to stop?

"What about you?" he asked. "You own the clothing store?"

"Yes. A dream come true, you might say. Perhaps not as adventurous as riding animals with attitude, but I like it."

"I don't know. There's something to be said for dealing with creatures who don't talk back."

As they fell into silence again, India noticed the rain was lessening in intensity. By the time a few more seconds ticked by, the worst of the storm had passed and she could see beyond the windshield again.

When Liam started the truck's engine, India wondered if he was as anxious to get out of their awkward situation as she was. After all, she'd bet it wasn't every day that he swept a potential business associate up into his arms. The image of him even attempting that with some big, burly cowboy had her stifling a giggle.

"Something funny?"

"No, nothing." She was saved from further questioning by her ringing phone. She pulled it from her purse and noted it was Verona. "Hey."

"Hey yourself, sweetie. Have you met with Mr. Parrish yet?"

"Yes, actually we're heading back to the shop now."

"Oh, good. Can you swing by the tourism office? Blake talked to the board, and we think we can iron out the details this afternoon if Mr. Parrish is agreeable."

India glanced over at Liam, noting how his long fingers wrapped around the steering wheel as he drove back into the edge of downtown. "Hang on a second," she said to Verona then lowered the phone.

Liam looked her way for a moment as he made a turn. "Problem?"

"The head of the tourism bureau wants to meet with you while you're here, but now probably isn't a good time." She gestured toward his wet clothing.

He nodded toward the back of the cab. "I always travel with an extra set of clothes if you've got somewhere I can change."

She smiled at that. "I own a clothing store. I bet we can scrounge up a dressing room."

When he smiled back, the surge of blood in her veins pushed her heart into a couple of extra beats it wasn't used to. She pulled her gaze away from that smile and refocused her attention on the call, bringing the phone back up to her ear. "Give us a few minutes, and we'll swing by."

As Liam guided the truck into a parking space across the street from her store, the rain stopped completely. The sun was already making a reappearance as she slid out onto the sidewalk.

"Need help?" Liam asked as he rounded the front of the truck.

Trying not to blush at the idea of him carrying her across the street for all of Blue Falls to see, she shook her head. "I'm fine."

When she finally got inside the store and directed Liam toward the dressing rooms, India sank onto the stool behind the cash register, slipped off her shoes and dropped her forehead into her upturned hand. With him out of her sight, she took several deep breaths and tried to pull some common sense to the surface. This was nothing more than the combination of meeting a nice-looking man and the memory of Elissa's teasing about hot cowboys. Once she got this meeting with Blake over with and Liam headed back to Fort Worth, she could pull her frazzled self back together.

But what if they signed Liam's company and she had to see him again? Work with him?

Well, she'd know what to expect then. She'd wear sensible shoes and avoid rainstorms. And she'd have time to steel herself against his rugged good looks, to remind herself that he was not the type of man she'd imagined being with if she ever slowed down long enough to even think about a serious relationship. She wanted someone cultured, refined, who'd seen the far reaches of the world and who might travel to them all again with her.

Her fantasy man was definitely not a cowboy who was probably more at home with livestock than people.

The splat of wet clothing hitting the hardwood floor drew her attention, and she looked toward the line of dressing rooms before she considered the wisdom of doing so. Beneath the wooden slats of the door, she noticed a lump of clothes that had to be Liam's wet jeans and socks. Next to them stood his naked feet and legs.

Her breath caught when she thought about all the naked flesh that door was hiding. Wet, firm, naked male.

She startled so much when the front door of the shop opened that she almost slid off the stool. She closed her eyes against the image of Liam Parrish in his altogether, then opened them to meet Verona's gaze. Another blush zoomed up India's neck to her face, but she attempted to hide it in the process of standing.

Blake Magnusson, head of the Blue Falls Tourist Bureau, followed Verona through the front door.

"I thought we were coming by your office," India said to Blake.

Verona waved off India's words. "Made more sense for us to come here. You've got a business to run, and we don't want to take you away from it longer than we have to." There was a worrisome bit of devilish sparkle in Verona's eyes as she scanned the interior of the shop. "Did you hide Mr. Parrish somewhere?"

India clamped down on the desire to shift her gaze to the dressing rooms. "We got caught in the rain, and he's changing into some dry clothes."

Verona eyed India. "You don't seem to be too wet."

"I was able to get inside quicker." Thanks to two very strong arms that she'd swear she could still feel scorching her legs and back. Lordy, she needed a fan to cool herself down.

Thankfully, Liam emerged from the dressing area fully clothed, drawing Verona's attention away from her. India spared Liam only a glance, but it was enough to notice he'd exchanged his blue shirt for a green one and a dry pair of jeans. Attempting to push away thoughts of that peek at his naked legs, India moved to make the necessary introductions.

"Liam Parrish, this is Blake Magnusson, head of the Blue Falls Tourist Bureau."

The men shook hands before Liam shifted his attention to Verona.

"And this must be your sister," he said, glancing back at India for a moment before shaking Verona's hand.

"Oh, I like this one," Verona said, smiling widely. "Blake, hire him on the spot."

Liam smiled and even shot Verona a wink. It took India a moment to remember she should be saying something.

"Verona Charles, former head of the tourist bureau," India said. "Also known as the lady who hasn't really grasped the concept of retirement yet."

Verona made a dismissive sound. "Retirement's for old people."

"Well, nobody here fits that description," Liam said, further charming Verona.

"Mr. Parrish, if I were a younger woman, you'd be in trouble right now." Verona shot India a look that said while she might be too old for Liam, India definitely wasn't.

Geez, just what she needed—to be caught in the crosshairs of Verona's incurable desire to matchmake. She'd been called Blue Falls' own Cupid on more than one occasion.

"I hear you've been able to take a look at our facilities," Blake said, thankfully steering the conversation in a less "Oh, look how hot the cowboy is" direction.

"Yes, India was kind enough to show me around. I think with a few repairs and adjustments, and some good prize money for the riders, you could pull in a sizable crowd."

India directed the others toward the table where this whole rodeo idea had been hatched. Over the next half hour, they hammered out the details and came away with a verbal agreement pending the forthcoming written contract.

"I think this calls for a bit of celebration," Verona said as they wrapped up the discussion. "I'm thinking pie down at the Primrose."

"Sounds good to me," Liam said.

India guessed he'd have a bit more than pie, considering he'd been hungry for lunch when he'd arrived at the shop earlier. The grin on Verona's face left India conflicted. Part of her didn't want to leave Verona alone with Liam. Who knew what kinds of crazy ideas she might put in his head? But she'd spent about as much time in Liam Parrish's presence today as she could handle. She needed some time alone to detox from his way-too-sexy, fry-your-brains looks.

When India didn't walk toward the front door like the rest of them, Verona looked back at her. "Aren't you coming, dear? It'll probably be slow here this afternoon, anyway."

India shook her head. "No, you all go ahead. I'm expecting a delivery this afternoon." Which was true, but also a convenient way of getting out of the pie outing.

She thought she heard Verona heave a sigh, but she ignored it. If Verona could find a successful man who looked as if he could grace the cover of *GQ,* then that would be a different story. Yes, Liam Parrish was dead sexy, but she very much doubted they had anything in common other than being citizens of the great state of Texas.

Liam opened the door and allowed Blake and Verona to go out ahead of him. But then he hesitated before following them and met India's eyes. He held the door with one hand and his bag of wet clothes with the other. "It was nice to meet you. And thanks for the use of your dressing room."

"You, too, and no problem." She nodded toward the bag in his hand. "You might want to hang those up in your truck so they don't sour." Needing to escape his gaze, she dipped below the front counter to retrieve a couple of wire hangers. "Here. I've got more of these than I can use."

Liam took a step forward and accepted the hangers. "Thanks." After a momentary pause, he nodded. "I'll be in touch."

She nodded back then watched as he walked out the door, said something to Verona and Blake then crossed the street to drop off his clothes in his truck. She noticed he just tossed everything into the backseat, not taking the time to hang his wet clothes. She rolled her eyes and forced herself to look away, to refocus on the order form for some 1920s flapper-style fashions.

But no matter how much she tried to make herself focus on work, her thoughts kept going back to that glimpse of naked legs and the indisputable fact that the sexiest man she'd seen in a long time had been fully naked mere feet from her. And it didn't seem to matter that he was nothing like her dream guy.

LIAM'S STOMACH FELT AS IF it were going to consume itself by the time the waitress at the Primrose brought his plate of chicken-fried steak with a heaping order of fries. The coffee and stale doughnut he'd downed that morning as he left Fort Worth were long gone.

"Thank you," he said to the waitress.

She gave him a shy smile before leaving the table.

"Don't look now, but I think you have another fan," Verona said as she gestured toward the waitress.

"She's a waitress. Being friendly is how they make good tips." And what did she mean by "another," anyway? Was she referring to herself? Because she surely couldn't mean India. They'd parted on friendly terms, but he couldn't imagine a woman like her giving him a second glance. Well, maybe a glance but nothing remotely serious. He'd learned that the hard way.

Still, there had been that unexpected moment in the truck earlier.

"I think you underestimate your appeal, Mr. Parrish."

"Verona, let the man eat his lunch," Blake said, his voice part teasing, part gentle scolding.

Verona swatted Blake playfully on the arm, drawing a laugh from her successor at the tourist bureau.

Thankfully, the rest of their conversation veered toward the rodeo, life in Blue Falls and how the rain would barely make a dent in the rainfall deficit. But no matter how the conversation twisted and turned, he couldn't keep his mind from wandering back to India Pike. One would think he'd learned his lesson with women who wore dainty, hundred-dollar shoes and then were surprised when they didn't hold up to a little uneven terrain. Give him a good, solid pair of boots any day.

But damn if he couldn't get the image of her striking, pale blue eyes and wavy black hair down to her shoulders out of his mind. Not to mention the curves of her body as he'd held her in his arms. What had possessed him to pick her up like that, anyway?

"Can I get you all some dessert?" the waitress asked from his side almost as soon as he'd finished his last fry.

"What kind of pie do you have today, Gretchen?" Verona asked.

"Pecan, lemon, rhubarb and chocolate fudge."

"You all enjoy," Blake said as he stood. "I've got to get back to work."

Liam reached across the table to shake the man's hand again. When he was left with just Verona and the waitress, he had to resist the urge to fidget.

"None for me, thanks," he said.

"Now you can't leave your first visit to the Primrose without some of its famous pie," Verona said. "I think it's actually against the law."

Gretchen nodded her agreement. "At least a night in jail."

Knowing better than to try to defy two women who had their minds set, he said, "In that case, I'll take a slice of pecan to go. I've got to get back to Fort Worth."

He didn't know if he actually saw a flicker of disappointment on Gretchen's face or if Verona's suggestion of an attraction was making him see things that weren't there. Whatever it was, it was gone in the blink of an eye.

"And for you, Verona?" Gretchen asked.

"I feel like lemon today. And get me a slice of the chocolate fudge for India. It's her favorite."

Gretchen nodded and headed off to retrieve the pie.

"Too bad India couldn't join us," Verona said. "At least I can get her some pie for the work she's doing on the rodeo."

Liam made a noncommittal sound.

After Gretchen brought them their to-go boxes and Liam picked up the bill, they headed out the front door. Verona pulled out her phone and looked at the display.

"Oh, I'm sorry, but I have to run." She looked at the take-out containers in her other hand then glanced down Main Street. "Could you drop off India's pie on your way back to your truck?"

Liam got the sneaking suspicion he was being maneuvered, but Verona was just so nice as she did it. How could he say no without looking like a jerk? Besides, it would only take him a few extra seconds, and then he could hit the road north.

"Sure," he said as he took the box she offered.

Verona squeezed his free hand. "Thank you, dear. See you soon." And then she was off, almost as if she wanted to make sure she was gone before he could change his mind.

Liam stood on the sidewalk watching her hurry away and couldn't help but laugh. He was pretty sure if he looked up *dynamo* in the dictionary, Verona Charles's smiling photo would be right there next to the definition. With a shake of his head, he turned and started down the sidewalk.

The moment he stepped inside Yesterwear, that flowery, female scent hit him again. If he wasn't careful, he was going to go back to Fort Worth smelling like a bouquet. Thank goodness he didn't have to go to the office—or, heaven forbid, a rodeo.

India wasn't anywhere to be seen. He was about to just

set the pie on the front counter and leave when he heard a loud grunt from farther back in the store. Concerned that she might have managed to injure herself with no one around to help her, he strode past the changing area and racks of frilly clothes. More grunts, louder now, led him to the back of the building where he spotted India, now barefoot, shoving large boxes across the floor toward a storeroom.

"Need some help?"

India yelped so loudly that Liam couldn't help but laugh. Wrong move, judging by how she straightened and shoved her fists against her hips.

"Sorry, didn't mean to scare you," he said.

"I thought you were gone." And didn't she sound as if she wished he was.

He lifted the take-out container. "Verona asked me to drop off a piece of pie for you."

Her stance softened a little. "What kind?"

"Chocolate fudge."

"I swear it's that woman's aim to make me fat." That still didn't keep India from walking up to him and taking the container holding said pie.

"I don't think you have to worry about that."

He noticed she didn't meet his eyes as she uttered a quick thanks. As she took a step toward the front of the shop, he placed his pie on a low, glass-topped table in front of two cushy white chairs and headed toward the pile of boxes.

"What are you doing?"

He looked back at her over his shoulder. "Being chivalrous?"

Her eyebrows bunched together, eliciting a smile from him.

"Where do you want these boxes?"

"I can get them."

"I'm sure you can…with a lot of grunting."

When her mouth dropped, he laughed.

"Come on, just tell me where you want them. Then we can both enjoy our pie sooner." He hadn't meant to stay and eat with her, but he suddenly found the thought appealing. She seemed like a stubborn, independent woman, and he got the distinct impression he'd knocked her a little off-kilter today. Whatever that said about him, he kind of liked it.

With a sigh, she tossed her container of pie next to his. "Fine." She strode past him and pointed at the biggest box. "Put that one on the table in the back." She indicated a long table that took up the back of the storage room.

It only took Liam a couple of minutes to heft the half-dozen boxes to the spots India indicated. When he placed the last one on a lower shelf filled with shoe boxes, he turned back toward her as he dusted off his hands. "See, no time at all."

"Yes, you're very manly," she said with a roll of her eyes.

He resisted the urge to flex his biceps. Geez, he hadn't acted that stupid since he was halfway through his teens. He realized that India wasn't the only one off-kilter today.

India headed out of the room, stopping at a small fridge to retrieve some bottles of water. Then she went outside the door to slip on a pair of white flip-flops with some sort of poufy flower-looking thing on top of them.

"Those shoes look a little safer," he said.

"You'd be surprised. Unfortunately, I tend to be way klutzier than I'd like to be."

He followed her back to the front of the store, nabbing their pie containers and plastic forks along the way. He should leave before he did something really stupid, but he found himself slipping into a chair across from her at the same table where they'd met with Verona and Blake earlier.

"So, Verona's an interesting lady," he said as he dug in to his pie.

"Lord, what did she do now?"

He chuckled. "Nothing much. She just seems really full of life, which is a good thing."

"Don't let her hear you say that. The next thing you know, she'll have you at her beck and call and thinking you begged for the honor."

"So, you really like her."

India opened her own pie box. "She grows on you." She took a bite of pie and made an appreciative sound that went right to the part of him that was thankfully hidden by the top of the table.

She closed her eyes for a moment as she swallowed the bite. Did she not have any idea how sexy she looked right now?

"Verona's the aunt of one of my best friends, so she's sort of like a second mom to all of us. She'd do anything for us, but she also gets these wild ideas in her head like she knows our paths to true happiness, too."

"Well, she was right about one thing."

India looked up to meet his gaze. "What's that?"

He cut another piece of his pie and gestured with it on the end of the fork. "It would be a crime to visit the Primrose and not have a slice of pie."

Just as they finished their dessert and India stood to toss their containers and forks in the trash, a tall brunette breezed through the front door. She stopped in her tracks when she spotted Liam then shifted her curious gaze to India.

When he also looked at India, he thought he detected more embarrassment, like she'd shown earlier after he'd carried her to the truck. He took that as his cue to head home for real this time.

"I'll send the contract out in tomorrow's mail," he said as he stood and met India's lovely eyes.

"Sounds good," she said with a quick nod.

The devil inside him almost wanted to say something to make the color rise higher in her cheeks, but he bit down on that idea. He had to work with her in the coming days, and the last thing he needed was to say or do something that would make that working relationship uncomfortable for them both.

"Ma'am," he said to the new arrival, who had curiosity coming off her like waves of heat on a highway in July.

All the woman managed was a nod and a strangled "Hey" before he made his way out the door. Instead of simply sliding into the driver's seat of his truck, however, he took the time to retrieve his drying Stetson and plop it atop his head. Then he looked back across the street and noticed the brunette staring out of the boutique's front window. And she wasn't the only one.

He tapped the front brim of his hat and smiled at India. Though it was probably the height of stupidity, he was already looking forward to returning to Blue Falls.

"Who was that mighty fine speciman of hunkitude?" Elissa asked as she blatantly watched Liam cross the street, tap his hat and drive down Main Street.

"Liam Parrish, the head of the rodeo company we're using." India tried to keep her voice even and matter-of-fact, with no more feeling than if she were telling Elissa what color of paint she'd picked out for her bathroom.

"Mmm-hmm, just like I predicted—hot cowboys." Elissa unfortunately shifted her attention to her friend just as a rush of heat washed through India. "And I see you appreciated the eye candy."

"The only thing hot around here is me. I've been shoving around boxes that feel like they're filled with rocks instead of clothing." Granted, Liam did most of the heavy lifting. No, she couldn't think about Liam, especially not with Elissa watching her every facial expression.

"I know you have Mr. Perfect all picked out in that little brain of yours, but don't stand there and tell me you didn't notice that man was hot enough to fry bacon on."

India shrugged. "He's okay."

With a sound of exasperation, Elissa rounded the front counter and retrieved the phone book. She licked her thumb and started turning pages.

"What are you looking for?"

"Dr. Pinter's number, because you obviously are in dire need of some glasses."

India threw up her hands. "You're as bad as Verona."

Elissa closed the phone book and smiled wide. "She's already set her sights on you, huh?"

India sat back at the table where she and Liam had eaten their pie. "Much to my dismay. As if putting me in charge of a rodeo wasn't bad enough, now she seems to think Liam is perfect for me."

"Maybe he is."

India gave her friend a long-suffering look. "You're just glad she's aiming her matchmaking efforts toward someone besides you."

Elissa leaned her forearms against the glass top of the jewelry display case. "Guilty as charged. From this vantage point, I can enjoy watching her make you squirm."

"I'm going to remember that when she eventually has you in her sights."

"Honey, I don't slow down enough for her to catch me."

"You live with her. How is that possible?"

"I'm good."

India snorted.

"Be careful not to snort in front of the gorgeous Mr. Parrish. You might run him off."

"Good. The last thing I need is a dusty cowboy tracking up my store." And her life.

"He didn't look dusty to me."

"Then you go out with him."

"Oh, no. I don't horn in on my friends' guys."

"Oh, for heaven's sake, he's not my guy. We've had this conversation a million times. I'm not interested in getting involved with anyone right now. I'm too busy. And even if I were looking, I wouldn't be looking toward someone like Liam." No matter how good-looking he was. No matter how he'd shown her more than once that chivalry wasn't dead.

"I know, you want James Bond without the danger."

"Well, thanks for making that sound deadly dull."

"You and Skyler need to live a little."

"Elissa, I love you like a sister, but lay off, okay? You know how much this store means to me, and how much work it takes to make a small business successful."

Elissa threw up her hands. "Fine, I'll hush."

"Thank you."

"But you can't blame me for saying 'I told you so' when you find working side by side with the sexy Mr. Parrish proves distracting."

India pointed at her friend. "I swear, I'm going to find a pocket-protector-wearing accountant and convince him that you're madly in love with him."

Elissa, blast her, just wiggled her eyebrows. "If he's cute underneath all the geek, I just might enjoy convincing him to shed the pocket protector."

India shook her head. "I'm so going to laugh myself into stomach cramps when you fall hard for some guy."

"You, too, missy. You, too."

And damned if Liam Parrish's sexy smile didn't take up residence in India's mind and refuse to vacate the premises.

Chapter Three

"So what do you think?" India asked Keri Teague after she finished pitching her idea for a cupcake contest as one of the activities to accompany the rodeo. "We're trying to get a wide variety of offerings so that people who might otherwise skip the rodeo will come out."

"It's a good idea," Keri said. "We'll need to do blind judging. I'm not about to take the heat for telling some little grandma that her cupcake recipe didn't win the blue ribbon."

India laughed. "Good point. So, what, maybe three judges?"

"That should be enough. And then we can sell the cupcakes after the judging is over. I can put some entry forms in the bakery."

"That would be great. Thanks." India glanced out the front window of Yesterwear for what felt like the millionth time.

"Something wrong?" Keri asked.

India jerked her attention back to Keri, owner of the popular Mehlerhaus Bakery and new wife to Sheriff Simon Teague. "Sorry. Just have so many things going on that I feel like there's a constant to-do list running in my brain." No way was she admitting that one of those items was watching for Liam Parrish to roll into town. As small as

Blue Falls was, that snippet would get back to Elissa and Verona before the sun set.

There really was no reason for him to come by the shop before heading to the fairgrounds to oversee the preparations for the rodeo, but that didn't keep her from jumping every time the front door opened or looking out the window whenever she heard a truck. She mentally shook her head. This was Texas. Everyone and their dog had a truck.

"I know what you mean. Speaking of, I better get back to the bakery. I've got a five-tier wedding cake covered with fondant songbirds to make this afternoon."

"I'll take unboxing a new shipment of hats any day."

Keri laughed, waved and was out the door. But the idea of that cake left India hungry. Deciding to take advantage of the lull in what had been a busy Thursday, she flipped the sign on the front door to say she'd return in fifteen minutes, locked up and headed down the sidewalk toward the Primrose Café.

Despite telling Elissa the previous week that she wasn't interested in Liam, she nevertheless found herself scanning the café's parking lot for his black pickup truck. She breathed a sigh of relief when she didn't see it. At least that's what she told herself. If she were being honest, their limited time together had generated a couple of very nice dreams.

After the dream the night before, she hadn't been able to go back to sleep. Instead, she'd gotten up and started digging through the wooden chest at the end of her bed. Beneath the handmade quilts, she'd rifled through the few keepsakes she'd kept from a childhood she largely wanted to forget. Below the high school yearbooks and the box containing the sash she'd worn after being crowned the Belle of Blue Falls, she found the old manila folder she'd been looking for, the one filled with magazine clippings of handsome guys and articles about successful businessmen in fields she admired. She forced herself to look through every piece of paper, reminding herself of how she'd always dreamed of a man as opposite to her deadbeat father as she could get.

Not that Liam Parrish was a deadbeat. He obviously wasn't since he owned his own company. Still, she got the impression that at heart he was a wandering rodeo cowboy. She couldn't imagine him eating at a café in Paris with a view of the Eiffel Tower or hiking through the Scottish Highlands or building schools in rural villages for girls who would otherwise not get an education. No, Liam was more than likely a "what you see is what you get" sort of guy, and she wanted a man with many layers, one who got more interesting and sexier with each layer that was exposed.

India ordered a chef salad to go, and she somehow found the willpower to resist caving in to the desire for a slice of fudge pie. Would she ever be able to eat her favorite dessert again without thinking of Liam? She half wished she hadn't come up with the rodeo idea in the first place, but hopefully it was going to generate a lot of money to help little Mia and her dad. India figured she could handle a bit of unexpected and unwanted attraction to Liam. After all, it was nothing compared to what Mia was going through.

Plus, after the rodeo was over, chances were she'd never see Liam again. She could get back to life as normal and let time and distance erode the memory of him.

After Gretchen handed over the salad, India headed back to the store in case the afternoon was as busy as the morning. She'd taken several steps across the Primrose's parking lot when she spotted a familiar black pickup. She nearly tripped over her own feet as she watched Liam slide out of the driver's seat. Damn, why did he have to do such nice things for a pair of jeans? He almost made her forget that she preferred stylish suits to jeans and scuffed cowboy boots, which were a dime a dozen in the heart of Texas. Didn't she?

After a deep, fortifying breath, India resumed her trek back to work. She didn't alter her path even though it would take her right past Liam. It wasn't as if she could avoid him in the days ahead, so she might as well just get used to seeing him now. Maybe the infatuation would actually fade if she talked to him more.

"Hey, Liam," she said as she drew close. See, that wasn't so hard.

But then his eyes met hers, and they widened the slightest bit. It was enough to make her wonder why. Had she simply surprised him, or was there something more there?

Now she was just being crazy. If she thought she had nothing in common with him, chances were he felt the same. She'd seen the deer-in-headlights look he'd worn when he'd stepped foot into Yesterwear the first time, as if he'd fallen through a hole into a different world. She'd seen it before on the faces of the men whose wives or girlfriends dragged them into the shop.

"India," Liam finally said after a moment's hesitation. He glanced at the box in her hand. "That's a big slice of pie."

"Actually, it's salad. I'm being good today."

"What a shame."

Heat flooded India's extremities, and she tried to tell herself that it was because of the midday heat. It couldn't be because Liam had meant anything other than it was a shame she wasn't going to enjoy a slice of pie. Her brain had trouble coming up with an appropriate response, but she was saved when Liam's attention shifted to the back of his truck.

A little girl with a dark brown ponytail stepped up beside him. It took a moment for the pieces to click into place. The girl's eyes were what clinched it.

"This must be your daughter," India said.

Liam placed one of his hands atop the girl's head with such affection that India actually hurt inside. She'd never had that kind of fatherly love, and no matter how old she got she never seemed to find a way to stop missing what might have been.

"Yes, this is Ginny, embarking on her first day of summer vacation by hanging with the old man. Ginny, this is India Pike. She's the one in charge of the rodeo here."

Ginny's forehead scrunched into furrows. "Really?"

"Ginny," Liam said in a warning tone.

A second or two passed before India laughed.

"I'm sorry," Liam said, looking at India with apology written all over his face.

"No, it's okay. She's got it pegged. After all, it is pretty absurd when you look at me."

"Still," Liam said as he gently tugged Ginny to his side and playfully mussed her hair. "We don't need to always say what we think."

"Sorry," Ginny said. Her crooked smile made her even cuter than she was on first glance.

"It's okay." India leaned forward and used her hand to pretend to block her words from Liam. "Any chance you want the job of running this rodeo?"

Ginny giggled, causing India to smile.

India glanced at Liam, and he had a smile on his face, as well. Lord, what was she doing? She should be maintaining a professional distance from him, not ingratiating herself with his young daughter.

"You have the number for the workers who are going to make the upgrades at the fairgrounds?"

Liam nodded. "We're meeting them after we grab some lunch."

"Good. If there's anything else you need, you have the number of the shop. I'll be there until later this afternoon."

"Swing by when you close up. I'll be able to show you how things are going."

Just when she thought she might get away with seeing him only once today… India's nerves sparked, but she refused to let her purely physical reactions get the better of her. She just had to ride them out until they faded and common sense took over.

"See you then." She shifted her gaze to Liam's daughter. "Nice to meet you, Ginny."

"You, too."

Anxious to get away, back to the familiarity of work, she gave Liam a nod and headed down the street without looking back.

Despite telling herself that she needed to shove aside attraction to Liam in favor of detached professionalism, India found herself fighting a losing battle throughout the afternoon. And she wasn't even where she could see him. It didn't help that the number of customers coming into the shop decreased significantly thanks to the increasing heat outside. She kept busy rearranging displays in the front window, pricing her new shipment of stock and creating an entry form for the cupcake contest.

But nothing she did kept her from looking at the clock what felt like every three seconds. As closing time drew near, she wondered if she should just stay at the store, continuing on until it got dark and the work at the fairgrounds was wrapped up for the day.

India stopped folding decorated flare jeans that screamed the 1970s and shoved her hands onto her hips. This wasn't her, not facing things head-on. If she'd made a habit of this kind of behavior, she never would have pulled herself out of poverty, gotten an education and come back to the town she loved but where there were at least some people who wouldn't have been surprised if she never amounted to anything.

She shook her head and finished folding the jeans. She always made a point to do her job well. That meant she would make sure the rodeo and accompanying activities were as successful as possible. To make that a reality, she couldn't avoid the man tasked with ensuring they had a successful rodeo.

When closing time came, India looked down at what she was wearing—a blue-and-white gingham top, white capri pants and denim ballet flats—and deemed the outfit safe for a trip to the fairgrounds. No heels to break off.

The butterflies in her stomach returned when she arrived at the fairgrounds. She gathered her courage and got out of her car. The thunking of hammers on wood drew her to the side of the arena. There she found local handyman Len Goodall and his teenage son, Adrian. Len looked up from where he was replacing a board on the fence surrounding the arena.

"Hey, India. You looking for Liam?"

"Yeah."

He gestured with his hammer toward the far end of the arena.

"Thanks." She picked her way over the crunchy, brown grass. When the rodeo came around, they'd have to keep the dirt settled in the arena with water or nobody would be able to see any of the events. They'd be too busy choking on the dust kicked up by the animals.

She rounded the end of the arena just in time to see Liam pause in his work on a gate to wipe the sweat on his shirtsleeve. Gone was the button-up he'd had on earlier. In its place was a white T-shirt that sported a picture on the back of a huge fish being pulled from the water by a fishing hook. She shuddered at the memory of the one time she'd gone fishing with her dad. She'd hated touching the worms they used as bait, couldn't make herself put them on the hooks, and was seriously creeped out by the slimy feeling of the fish.

"Hey," he said when he finally spotted her.

Just relax. "Hey. Looks like a hot job."

Liam glanced at the gate that led into the arena. "Yeah, but I'm just about done. Actually, if you'll help me, I've only got one more board to attach."

She gave him an "Are you crazy?" look. "I'm not exactly dressed for manual labor."

He smiled as he took in what she wore. "Oh, I don't know. Looks way more sensible than what you wore here the last time."

She shook her head. "What do you need?"

He picked up a board and settled it against the frame of the wooden gate. "If you'll just hold one end steady, this will only take a moment."

India was careful not to brush against the gate with her white pants as she held the board with one hand and steadied the gate with the other.

True to his word, a few quick strikes of the hammer and Liam had the opposite end affixed. When he turned and grabbed the end she held, his warm hand grazed hers. It was only a momentary touch, but it was enough to cause India's breath to catch. She feared he noticed it when he looked up and his eyes met hers.

He was close, much too close. As casually as she could, she released the board and took a couple of steps away. "Looks like you all have gotten a lot done today."

"Yeah, we'll be done with the arena repairs by Monday." Liam finished attaching the new board before he came to stand next to her, propping one booted foot on the bottom slat of the gate. "We'll paint after that, then get the barns ready to hold the animals."

She glanced toward him as he pushed his hat back off his forehead. He was sweaty and dirty, and that should have turned her off. Instead, it was having the opposite effect.

"I thought you were here just to supervise," she said.

"I'm not the type to stand around doing nothing," he said. "I'd be bored out of my mind. Plus, this way we get things done quicker, and it costs you all less money."

Why did he have to sound so reasonable, so nice? Why couldn't he just be a dumb lug who had nothing appealing about him but a good-looking face? It'd be so much easier for her to stop thinking about him then.

She let her gaze roam over the entirety of the fair-grounds, picturing how they would set up the vendor booths. At the far end of the grassy area, she spotted a large, black horse with a short rider. It took her a moment to realize it wasn't an adult.

"Is that Ginny?"

"Yeah. She's letting Inky stretch her legs after being cooped up in the trailer for several hours."

"That animal is huge. Don't you worry she'll get hurt?"

"Ginny's been on horseback since before she could walk. That's how it goes when your dad is a rodeo rider."

India barely knew the child, so the surge of anxiety over seeing her astride such a powerful animal surprised her.

"Hey, maybe Ginny can teach you to ride," Liam said.

India started shaking her head before Liam even finished speaking. "Oh, no. I'm not getting anywhere near that animal. Horses can sense that I'm scared to death of them."

"You've really never been on a horse?"

India shifted her attention away from where Ginny seemed to be effortlessly maneuvering the horse. "Nope. And I don't intend for that to change any time soon."

She liked her life just like it was, with everything mapped out. She wasn't as married to perfectionism as Skyler, but India still knew what fit her lifestyle and what didn't. Running a rodeo and learning to ride a horse had never been on her radar screen.

But neither had a sweaty, dirty cowboy who tempted her to second-guess what she'd always known she wanted.

"REMIND ME AGAIN WHY I'm friends with you," Skyler said as she dragged herself out of the car after India and Elissa. "This is a heinous hour for human beings to be up."

India smiled at her friend, who'd never been an early riser. "Because we need to measure for the booth spaces, and I'd like to do it before it's a thousand degrees outside."

"Plus there are those little things called jobs we all have to go to later," Elissa said. Unlike Skyler, Elissa was quite fond of early mornings.

Skyler stuck her tongue out at both of them, eliciting laughs from her best friends.

"You all certainly sound happy this morning."

India halted in her tracks and jerked her gaze toward the sound of the male voice. Liam—and his deep, sexy voice—sat in a lawn chair beside the RV she'd seen the day before.

"Oh, hey. I didn't think anyone would be out here yet," India said. In fact, she'd been banking on it. But it looked as if Liam was using the RV as more than an on-site office. "Sorry if we bothered you."

"Not at all. Just enjoying a cup of coffee before it gets too hot outside to drink it." He lifted a cup. "Would you all like some?"

"No, we're fine," India said.

"Actually, I'd love some coffee," Elissa said. She shot India a grin that said India was in trouble. "And Skyler might be a little nicer if we get some caffeine in her."

India stared hard at Elissa, silently promising payback, before her friend shifted her gaze and walked toward Liam as he stood. She extended her hand. "I'm Elissa. I'm the fun friend in this motley trio."

Liam laughed as he accepted Elissa's hand, gifting her with a smile even wider than any he'd aimed in India's direction.

Something greedy churned inside India, making her want to break the contact between Elissa and Liam. Her jaw clenched before she forced herself to relax. Truth be told, Liam was more up Elissa's alley, anyway. She obviously found him attractive. And if he didn't think Elissa was drop-dead gorgeous, then he was blind.

Once they finished shaking hands, Elissa gestured toward Skyler. "This is Skyler, but you can call her I Don't Do Mornings." When Elissa gestured toward India, she noticed the conspiratorial grin she wore as she and Skyler made eye contact. "And you've met Fuddy Duddy."

"Fuddy Duddy?" India crossed her arms. "I fail to see how I deserve that nickname."

Liam put up his hand, palm out. "I'll leave the nicknames to you ladies and get your coffee."

When Liam disappeared into the RV, India eyed Elissa. "What are you doing?" she asked under her breath.

"Being friendly."

India bit her lip. She knew that Elissa being friendly usually led to her going out on a date. Her friend didn't sleep around, but she knew how to have a good time. And India had never heard any of Elissa's dates complain, either.

"Damn, he's even hotter in person," Elissa said.

"Shh." India shot a nervous glance toward the RV's open doorway.

"What? It's true. He's got to know it. I'd venture a guess

that even Skyler noticed, half-asleep as she is. Right, Skyler?"

"He's not exactly ugly."

"Oh, my God, I can't believe you two." India turned on her heel and headed away from them. She was tempted to get in her car and leave them behind. They could think about the wisdom of pushing her in a direction she didn't want to go while they walked back to their cars downtown.

Instead of abandoning her friends, however, she retrieved the tape measure and notepad from the car. She eyed the ground for a rock to place on one end of the tape since her friends seemed to be more interested in drinking coffee and ogling the hot cowboy.

She gritted her teeth, more irritated with herself than Elissa and Skyler. If she had her sights set on a man she hadn't yet met, why did she care if Elissa or even Skyler found Liam attractive?

"Looks like you could use a hand," Liam said as he approached.

She gestured toward where her friends were sipping their mugs of fresh coffee. "That's what I brought them for, but that didn't turn out as planned."

"Have I done something to offend you?"

India stopped searching for a rock and met Liam's gaze. She shook her head and allowed the tension building in her shoulders to relax. "No, I'm sorry. I guess Skyler isn't the only one grumpy this morning." She pulled out the end of the measuring tape and extended it to Liam. "I think I'm just letting my to-do list get the better of me."

Liam took the end of the tape and held it as she started walking backward, away from him and her friends. "Anything I can help with?"

"I think you already have your plate full, too."

"You never know. I might be able to squeeze something else in."

India glanced toward Liam, but despite the fact that he wasn't yet wearing his hat she couldn't read his expression. Was there some innuendo there, or was she just imagining it thanks to Elissa's teasing?

"I'll be fine, but thanks."

"Okay, but the offer stands."

She wondered how he'd respond if he knew that the kind of help she imagined him giving her had absolutely nothing to do with the rodeo.

Chapter Four

Even while measuring out spaces for vendor booths, India looked like a flower in the middle of the desert. Liam wasn't normally prone to think of things in such a, well, flowery way, but it was the first thing that had popped into his mind when he'd seen her standing alone in the middle of the dry field. She looked so out of place that it should have sounded warning bells in his head. Big, clanging bells.

He should just do his job here and beat it back to Fort Worth as quickly as he could. But no, what did he do? He offered to help her with some unnamed task just because she looked stressed and he wanted to smooth away the lines on her beautiful face.

India wrote down her last measurement then started walking toward him. "Thanks for the help."

"No problem."

She looked past him toward the female chattering. "Looks like we woke up Ginny, and she's already making friends with my coffee-mooching friends."

He looked back to where Ginny was sitting cross-legged in the chair he'd vacated. "That kid has never met a stranger. I'm afraid it's going to come back to bite me in the butt one of these days. She gets older and I'll be beating off cowboys with whatever is handy."

"She spends a lot of time with you?"

He could tell there was a question beyond the question, but India was better than most about hiding it. "Ginny lives with me full-time. Her mother isn't a part of her life."

"Oh. I didn't mean to pry."

He shrugged. "You weren't."

"That must be hard when you're on the road so much."

"She stays with my cousin when I'm out of town during the school year, but she travels with me during the height of rodeo season."

"Really? That must be pretty lonely for her."

He laughed. "Remember what I said about her not meeting a stranger? I think she knows every rider, announcer, stock handler and clown on the circuit."

"I just meant she's probably the only kid."

He hadn't really thought about that before. After all, Ginny never complained. In fact, she seemed to enjoy their time on the road. He turned his gaze back to his daughter and for the first time wondered if he was doing her a disservice by dragging her from one rodeo to another.

He shook his head. No, Ginny had a good life. She loved horses, loved rodeos. Why was he letting this woman who reminded him a little too much of Charlotte put doubts in his head? He knew his daughter better than anyone. And just because India Pike would probably turn a daughter of hers into a little cream puff didn't mean that was right for Ginny.

"Time for me to get to work." He didn't even look at India when he started back toward the RV.

"I see you all got everything taken care of," Elissa said.

"No thanks to you lazy bums," India said as she strode up next to him. Her voice and posture were tight again, like they'd been when she'd first arrived.

His abrupt change in mood had probably caused that, but he couldn't muster feeling sorry this time. He didn't need any parenting advice from someone who didn't even have a kid. At least he didn't think India had any children. She didn't strike him as the motherly type. She was way too uptight for that. Plus, if she had kids, she wouldn't always look like she'd walked out of a fashion catalog. Really, who looked that good this early in the morning?

Someone like Charlotte. A woman who didn't have the first clue about the kind of life he lived and probably never would.

He refocused on his daughter, ruffling her serious case of bedhead. "Did you sleep in a wind tunnel last night?"

She gave him one of her "I'm just putting up with you because you're my dad" looks.

"Ginny was just keeping us entertained with a story about you and a horse named Jumping Bean," Elissa said with laughter in her voice.

Elissa was pretty, laid-back, casual, funny. Why couldn't he be attracted to her instead of her rose petal of a best friend?

"Glad to know she's sharing that tale with everyone she meets." He acted as if he was going to tickle Ginny's ribs, but she squealed as she jumped out of the chair and ran from him.

As luck would have it, she ended up hiding behind India, who looked startled by suddenly being Ginny's main line of defense.

"This must be one doozy of a story," India said as she glanced down to where Ginny was peeking around India's waist, a glint of victory in her little-girl eyes.

"Evidently not only did the horse buck Liam off in no time flat," Elissa said, obviously reveling in the retelling, "but he came back and bit Liam on the posterior to add insult to injury."

He watched as India did her best to hide a smile. He had

to resist the sudden, very unwise urge to grab her and kiss that grin right off her face.

This job couldn't be over fast enough.

"COME ON, DON'T BE MAD," Elissa said as she followed India through the front door of Yesterwear.

India walked to her small office and tossed her purse in the bottom drawer of the desk. "I'm not mad. More like irritated. You're like a mosquito that won't stop buzzing around my ear."

"What? All I did was invite Liam and Ginny to family night at the music hall."

"After making a point that I'd be there."

"I said we'd all be there, along with a lot of other people, including some kids Ginny could meet."

India pushed past Elissa on her way back to the front of the store. "It was obvious what you meant."

"So shoot me for trying to set up one of my best friends with the best-looking guy to stroll into Blue Falls in ages."

India spun back toward Elissa and the wisely quiet Skyler. "I'm perfectly capable of choosing my own dates."

Elissa crossed her arms and cocked an eyebrow. "Really? And just when exactly did you last go on a date?"

India exhaled in exasperation. "I'm a busy woman. I'll get around to it." She gestured toward Skyler. "Why don't you shift your matchmaking efforts toward Skyler?"

"Hey, leave me out of this."

"I have to work up to Skyler. That'll take more work. She's even more uptight than you are."

"On that lovely note, I'm going to work," Skyler said and headed for the door. "You two try not to kill each other."

Once the door closed behind Skyler, India glanced at Elissa. "Don't you need to get to work, too?" She wanted nothing more than to be alone. Just five glorious minutes without having to avert her eyes from a guy she shouldn't want, or listen to her friends try to map out her future for her.

"You're right." Elissa's words were unusually clipped, and India fought the urge to apologize.

Only she wasn't the one who'd done anything wrong. She didn't go around trying to run Elissa's life, setting her up with a guy with whom she had absolutely nothing in common, a guy who would only be in town for a short time, anyway. When India got involved with someone, she wanted to make sure he was going to be around for a while.

But how likely was it that the type of man she'd always told herself she wanted was going to take up residence in Blue Falls? Would she have to leave to find him? Leave her friends, the business she loved and the town that felt more like home than the house she'd shared with her parents ever had?

A sudden fear that she would lose it all swamped her just as Elissa grabbed the knob on the front door.

"I'll call you later, when I get some more of the plans for the rodeo activities finished," India said.

"Fine." Without even looking back, Elissa disappeared in the opposite direction from Skyler.

India couldn't decide if she wanted to scream or cry.

LIAM TOOK OFF HIS GLOVES and beat the dust off of them on one of the barn's support beams. Half of the load of hay was spread in the stalls that they'd spent the day repairing and prepping for horses. He caught Adrian's gaze as the boy entered the end of the barn with two bottles of water fresh from the icy cooler.

"You read my mind," Liam said as he accepted one of the dripping bottles. "I feel like I've eaten one of these bales of hay."

Adrian laughed then took a deep gulp of water.

"So, this music hall," Liam said, trying to sound casual. "Lots of people go there?"

"Yep, always packed. Only thing you could really call nightlife in Blue Falls. And tonight's family night, the one night of the week when they don't serve alcohol so people can bring their kids. You should check it out. Good way to meet the neighbors, even if they are temporary."

Liam shrugged. "Maybe. I'm not sure a shower and going to bed early doesn't sound better."

This time it was Adrian's turn to shrug.

Liam looked back over everything they'd accomplished today. "Go tell your dad to pack it in. I think we've all sweated enough buckets for one day."

"Okay. Maybe we'll see you later at the music hall."

Liam just grunted in response since Adrian was already halfway to the barn opening. He wasn't sure taking Elissa up on her offer was such a good idea. But on the other hand, he and Ginny deserved a night out. Ever since India had put that doubt in his head about taking Ginny on the road with him, he'd caught himself watching his daughter for signs of boredom, loneliness or just wishing she was anywhere else. Things he might have not even noticed before seemed to jump out and scream at him. Part of him hated India for that, but only a little part.

What was more frustrating was the fact that a bigger part wanted to go to the music hall tonight just to see what she'd wear. Would she even show up? Yes, she was a local and evidently a lot of the locals frequented the Blue Falls Music Hall, but as much as he tried he couldn't imagine her there. A classical concert hall, yes. A Texas music hall filled to the rafters with cowboy boots and country music, not so much.

With a shake of his head, he headed back to the RV. He

wasn't lying when he'd said a shower sounded really good. He scanned the fairgrounds as he crossed the space between the barn and where the RV was hooked up, but he didn't see Ginny anywhere. When he stepped inside the cooler interior of the RV, he saw why. She was lying on his bed with her bare feet propped against the wall, reading.

"Good book?"

She nodded. "Yeah, I've read it before." Was that a hint of boredom in her voice?

He didn't much feel like going out, but he decided that it might be good for Ginny to meet some of the local kids. "What do you think about going to this music hall Elissa mentioned?"

Ginny tossed the book aside and spun around to a sitting position on the edge of the bed. "Could we?"

He laughed even though a little part of him suddenly felt like crying. Maybe India was right, even though he hated to admit it. What kind of father was he that a complete stranger had guessed something about his daughter that he'd overlooked for who knew how long?

"Well, go on, then, and take a quick shower. But don't use all the hot water."

Ginny flew to the bathroom. When she closed the door, he slumped onto one of the benches next to the dining table. He was going to be a better dad from now on. He didn't know much about girly things, but he'd figure it out. Ginny was the most important thing in the world to him, and he wasn't going to mess that up.

By the time they both showered, dressed and stopped by the Primrose for some dinner, the music hall was indeed doing a brisk business. Couples spun around the dance floor, more people stood in groups around the room talking and laughing, and several kids sat at the bar with their short legs swinging off the tall stools.

Liam placed his hand on Ginny's shoulder. "Looks like they have ice cream. You want some?"

"Yes!" She threw her arm in the air as if celebrating a major victory.

When they reached the bar, Ginny scrambled up onto the only empty bar stool. That's when Liam noticed Verona behind the bar scooping ice cream. A moment after he noticed her, she looked up and met his gaze. A wide smile spread across her face.

"Look what the cat dragged in," Verona said.

"You really don't take this retirement thing very seriously," Liam said over the sudden clapping for the band playing.

"Oh, this? I'm just lending a hand. There's usually two gals working back here, but one of them had her wisdom teeth out today. I'm guessing she's got a hot date with her painkillers tonight." Verona shifted her gaze to Ginny. "Is this your sister?"

Ginny giggled. "No. He's my daddy."

"Oh, he is? Do you think your daddy will let you have some ice cream?"

"Yes."

"Yes, what?" Liam said.

"Yes, please."

Verona smiled again. "Now what kind of ice cream can I get for a young lady with such fine manners?"

"Strawberry, please."

"Strawberry it is."

As Verona turned away to scoop the ice cream, Liam let his gaze wander over the crowd. He could tell himself he wasn't looking for India, but that would be a lie. Maybe fate was kinder than his hormones tonight because he didn't see her anywhere.

"I see you decided to take me up on my suggestion."

Liam turned his head and noticed Elissa had walked up next to him while he wasn't looking, Skyler not far behind.

"Yeah. Looks like you were right about it being popular."

He pushed away a shot of disappointment that the trio of friends appeared to be a person short.

"I think India skipped out on us tonight."

Liam detected a layer of irritation in Elissa's voice, but he dared not comment on it.

Suddenly, a guy grabbed Elissa's hand and dragged her, laughing, toward the dance floor. She shot a wave back toward Liam but was quickly lost in the mass of dancers.

"I think I had that much energy once, when I was about twelve," he said.

"Yeah, that's our Elissa. Never a dull moment." Skyler took a sip of what appeared to be a soda of some sort.

For a moment, Liam remembered those early, carefree days when he'd been on the rodeo circuit, before he'd slept with Charlotte, before she'd shown up at the rodeo in Cheyenne and handed him a baby along with papers giving up her parental rights. He'd barely been able to get ten words out before she'd turned tail and run. Though it had been the biggest shock of his life, now he couldn't imagine his life without Ginny. Things might not have always been perfect, but he thought they'd made it work okay.

A flash of red across the room pulled him from his mental wanderings through the past.

Ginny spun around on the stool with her bowl of ice cream. She pointed right where he'd been looking. "Look, there's India."

There was no way he could have missed her. She wore a red dress and black heels that reminded him of the women in those old World War II movies.

Beside him, Skyler waved to get India's attention. Instead of looking at Skyler, however, India's eyes met and held his for a long moment before she looked to her left and said something to a guy who'd spoken to her. Liam had the sudden, burning urge to toss the guy out the front door on his head.

Hell, he was losing his mind if he was being tempted to fall back into the same trap again. After all, he remembered vividly the first time he'd seen Charlotte, too. Like India, she'd definitely stood out in a crowd, a shiny penny among a bunch of dull nickels.

Needing to look anywhere but at her, Liam turned toward the bar. "I think I'll take some ice cream myself."

"Flavor?" Verona asked, her mouth twitching at the edge as if she knew exactly what he was doing.

"Rocky Road." Now didn't that just describe his life right now?

INDIA NEARLY TURNED ON HER heel and retraced her steps outside, especially when her gaze caught and held Liam's across the room. But that would negate the long talk she'd had with herself earlier. Just because he didn't fit her image of the perfect guy didn't mean she had to avoid Liam. She could be friendly, get to know him a little more, maybe even dance to a song or two if that opportunity presented itself. After all, it wasn't as if she was going to marry the guy.

She took a steadying breath then crossed the room to where Skyler was waving at her. A quick glance to the right as she passed the dance floor revealed Elissa laughing and having a good time with Greg Bozeman, Blue Falls' best mechanic and all-around good guy.

By the time she reached Skyler, Liam had turned his back. She didn't know if that made her feel better or worse.

"I didn't know if you'd come tonight," Skyler said so that no one else could hear her.

"I almost didn't."

"You know she's just trying to help in her own over-the-top way," Skyler said with a glance toward Elissa, then toward Liam.

"I know. But she should know once I've got my mind set on something, there's no changing it unless I want to change it."

"Proving that you and Elissa are both stubborn."

India bumped Skyler's shoulder. "I think there might be three of us in that pot."

"Must be why we're all such good friends."

Skyler's phone rang, and when she looked at the display she groaned.

"Work?"

Skyler nodded as she answered and started making her way toward the door so she could hear the caller on the other end.

"You're pretty."

It took India a moment to realize the person who'd spoken was Ginny, and that she was talking to her. And that Liam had noticed what his daughter had said.

"Thank you. You are, too, by the way."

Ginny smiled and extended her partially eaten bowl of ice cream. "Would you like some?"

A smile tugged at India's lips. "No, thank you, sweetie. You enjoy it." She looked up at Liam, and her smile faltered a little.

"Can I get you something to drink?" he asked.

She nearly said no, but she imagined Elissa's look of disappointment that she wasn't even trying to "live a little."

"A Coke would be great, thanks." She turned to Ginny and asked, "Are you enjoying yourself?"

Before Ginny could answer, someone grabbed India around the waist and pulled her toward the dance floor. "I'm about to enjoy myself," T. J. Malpin said as he breathed on her with his beer-scented breath. He leaned too close to her face. "Did I ever tell you how much I love red?"

India dug in her heels and tried to push away from him. "I'm not in the mood to dance, T.J."

"What, you think you're too good for me? Ain't that rich? Little poor girl done gone and got high-and-mighty."

India's face flamed, partly from embarrassment and partly in anger. She felt as if his words boomed so loudly that everyone in the music hall had heard them over the band and the thud of boots on the wooden dance floor. She'd gone to school with T.J., and when he wasn't drinking he was an okay guy. But get some alcohol in him, and he had a problem holding his tongue.

Tears pooled in her eyes as she tried to extricate herself without causing a scene. One moment he was hanging on to her waist, and the next he'd been ripped away.

"She said she didn't want to dance." Liam stood several inches taller than T.J., and the look on his face made India's heart beat a little faster.

"Who the hell are you?"

"The guy who's going to teach you some manners if you don't leave right now." The fierceness in Liam's voice didn't leave any doubt that he meant what he said.

India caught sight of Deputy Pete Kayne as he strode up beside Liam.

"Come on, T.J. It's time you and I go have a come-to-Jesus meeting."

Liam hung on to T.J. for the space of a couple more heartbeats before he finally let Pete escort T.J. and his foul breath out of the music hall. Then he turned his attention toward her.

"Are you okay?"

The intensity of Liam's concerned gaze frazzled India almost as much as T.J.'s drunken attention. Still, she managed to nod. "Yeah. He just surprised me." And dragged her back in time to a part of her life she'd worked very hard to put behind her. Had Liam heard him? How many other people?

Liam took her gently by the elbow and led her toward the bar. When she saw the wide-eyed concern on Ginny's face, India forced herself to smile as if nothing were wrong. Wanting to shift Ginny's attention in a different direction, India nodded at the now empty bowl in Ginny's hands.

"How was your ice cream?"

Ginny looked confused by the question for a moment before she answered. "Good. Who was that man?"

So much for diverting her line of thought.

"Oh, don't worry about that. He just wasn't feeling himself. He should be better in the morning." Well, except for the hangover and the fact that he might be waking up in a cell at the sheriff's department—again.

The band on stage tonight, local favorites the Teagues of Texas, wrapped up their first set with a flourish and announced they'd be back after a break. The house DJ put on some familiar country hits in their absence.

"Hey, I have an idea," India said. "Why don't you go dance with your dad?" Maybe that would give India time to recover from her encounter with T.J., and a break from the intense way Liam was still watching her, as if she might break at any moment.

India made the mistake of glancing at Liam, and she could tell by the look in his eyes that he knew exactly what she was doing, pushing him away and crawling further into her shell than she'd been in a long time. Still, he wasn't going to disappoint his daughter, so he let Ginny take his hand and lead him onto the dance floor.

They really were cute together with Liam twice Ginny's height, Ginny smiling from ear to ear and Liam twirling her through the song like he'd done it a thousand times before. Maybe he had. It was obvious Ginny thought her dad hung the moon. India wondered if maybe she'd been wrong when she suggested Ginny might be lonely on the rodeo circuit.

A pang of envy twisted in her middle. What was it like to look up at one's dad with such love and admiration? To have your dad make you feel as if you were the most important person ever, not just on the planet but in the universe?

Before India could even begin to relax, Elissa and Skyler approached her from both sides.

"Are you okay?" Elissa asked.

"Yes, fine." Really, she wished people would stop asking her that, would stop looking in her direction, would just forget it happened.

"I guess T.J. spent a little too much time at the Frothy Stein before he ventured over here," Skyler said. "I had to stifle a laugh when Pete got him outside. He smacked T.J. on the back of the head and told him what an idiot he was."

Any other time, the story would have been funny. Everyone in town had a story that involved T.J. and his best frenemy, Adam Parker. But tonight, thinking of T.J. and what he'd said just made India's stomach churn.

"Are you sure you're okay?" Elissa asked. "You look like you're going to be sick."

"Just tired. I think I'm going to go home."

"Don't let T.J. win like that," Skyler said.

"Yeah, the best thing to do to sweep this away is for you to act as if it didn't bother you. Stay and have some fun."

"They're right," Verona said from behind the bar. "You need to dance with that handsome cowboy before somebody else gets it in her mind to do so."

"I don't think I'm going to be the best company tonight." But did she really want to go home? Yes, she was embarrassed, but she knew what she'd do if she went home now.

She'd sit and let herself worry about a past she couldn't change.

"Well, no, because that's me, obviously," Elissa said.

Despite what had transpired over the past several minutes, India laughed then shook her head. "I love your modesty."

"I am nothing if not modest."

Verona snorted at that one, which set the rest of them to laughing.

Pete made his way back through the crowd only a few seconds before Liam and Ginny left the dance floor.

"Did you arrest that guy?" Liam sounded as if he'd like to give T.J. a good beat-down.

India knew she should be wary of that kind of violence, should say something about being able to take care of herself. After all, she'd been doing it for as long as she could remember. But there was a distinctly feminine part of her that liked having a guy willing to come to her defense.

"T.J. will be a guest of the county tonight," Pete said. "We really should start charging him rent."

"Okay, boys and girls," Simon Teague said from the stage. "We want to see everyone paired up and on the dance floor for this next one."

"You heard the man," Verona said. "Grab while the grabbing's good."

"Well, I can't disobey my boss and my next-door neighbor," Pete said as he grabbed Elissa and headed for the growing number of couples.

This time around, Greg Bozeman nabbed Skyler despite her protest that she'd been on her feet all day at the inn.

India's nerves sparked to life when she was left standing on the sidelines with Liam.

"Go on, you two," Verona said. "Don't be party poopers."

India glanced at Liam in time to see indecision flit across his face. "It's okay," she said. "We'll hang out with Ginny."

"Then you're going to have to go to the dance floor because I think she's going to have a partner in a moment," Verona said.

Liam's face tightened until he looked past Ginny to where Nathan and Grace Teague's son, Evan, was headed straight toward Ginny.

India had to hide a smile. "Hey, Evan."

He gave one of those enthusiastic, little-boy waves.

"Ginny, Liam, this is Evan Teague," India said. "That's his dad and uncles in the band."

Liam, relaxing, extended his hand to shake Evan's as if he were a grown-up. "Nice to meet you, Evan."

"Want some ice cream?" Ginny asked. "They've got all kinds."

"Sure."

This time Liam was trying to suppress a smile as Evan scrambled up onto the stool next to Ginny.

India took a step closer to Liam and leaned toward him. "You're not very good at hiding that you want to smile right now."

Liam turned his back to the kids. "If I don't get away from here right now, I'm going to start laughing and embarrass Ginny." He held out his hand. "Save me with a dance?"

India's breath caught and she had to force her lungs to start behaving properly again. With a nervous smile, she said, "Sure," and placed her hand in Liam's.

The moment his big hand wrapped hers in warmth, her knees weakened a bit. But this was just one dance, nothing more. Besides, he had helped her break free from T.J. and any further embarrassment he could have caused.

Her thought that this was merely a simple dance between budding friends faltered when he placed his arm around her back and pulled her close. The overwhelming maleness of him made it difficult to breathe, and when she finally did manage to take a breath she smelled him. A manly soap that reminded her of evergreens and some other scent that she couldn't name. She might not be able to identify it, but there was no mistaking one-hundred-percent, red-blooded male.

"Are you sure you're okay?"

"Yes, really. Do I look that fragile?"

"No, you look beautiful."

India lowered her gaze to the middle of Liam's chest and stared at one of the buttons. If she were a different sort of woman, she'd be tempted to start releasing those buttons to see what lay beneath.

Who was she kidding? She was tempted now.

"I didn't mean to embarrass you," he said, stirring the hair atop her head with his breath.

"You didn't. I...I've just had a long day. I probably should have gone home."

"I'm glad you didn't."

India missed a step, but Liam's grip on her tightened enough that she didn't fall, didn't even falter enough for anyone else to notice. No one, that was, but her.

She looked up into his eyes and felt as if she'd never seen anything more beautiful. The image of her perfect man faded some in her mind, gradually being replaced by Liam's angular face shaded by that ever-present cowboy hat. What was scariest was in this moment, with him holding her so close she could feel the warmth of his body, she didn't mind. Not one bit.

Chapter Five

Liam tightened his grip on India a fraction, enough that he hoped he could prevent her from bolting. Because that was what she was thinking about doing. He saw it in her eyes the moment he'd said she was beautiful, felt it in the increased tension in her body. But he didn't regret saying it, no matter how much his common sense was screaming at him not to go down that road. Because it was true. She was the most beautiful woman in the entire music hall. He couldn't figure out why every male eye in the place wasn't trained on her, but he was glad they weren't.

"Looks like Ginny does make friends pretty quickly," India said.

He pulled his gaze away from her to look over toward the bar. Verona said something as she slid more ice cream in front of Ginny and Evan, and the kids burst out laughing.

"If Verona is trying to matchmake my kid, I'm going to have something to say about that."

There it was again, the slight tightening of her muscles. He guessed he'd just given himself away, that he knew that Verona was trying to push them together. He opened his mouth to say that she didn't have to worry. He didn't push women into relationships they didn't want. But he couldn't find the words because, honestly, there was a little part of him that wanted to find out what it would be like with

India. He wanted to believe she wasn't like Charlotte, but did it even matter?

India was fond of saying she was really busy. Well, he could claim the same thing. Running his business as well as still riding occasionally took up a lot of time. And the rest belonged to Ginny. She already had one parent who'd never given her a moment of her time. He wasn't about to do the same.

"She just loves kids," India said as she looked at Verona with genuine affection. "She's like the cool grandma to every little kid in Blue Falls."

"I've never seen a grandma with quite so much energy."

India laughed. "I know. She's always been that way. Skyler, Elissa and I are convinced the woman has more energy than all of us put together. It's very annoying sometimes."

Liam smiled. "But you love her."

India nodded. "Yeah. She's been like a second mother to us."

He sensed there was more to those simple words, but he didn't know India well enough to ask. But he suddenly wanted to. He could keep things simple, with no expectation of anything beyond his time here in Blue Falls. Of course, he couldn't just come right out and say that. She was way too skittish and withdrawn for that. For some reason, India Pike had walls built around her. And they'd gone up even further when that drunken jackass had manhandled her tonight. He'd wanted to punch the guy into another time zone.

The song was over much too quickly, and India was already pulling out of his arms as the final notes were played. She looked up at him with a smile that told him she was telling the truth, at least partially, about being tired.

"Thanks for the dance," she said. "And for the help with T.J. I'm sorry you got pulled into that."

"I wasn't pulled into anything, India. I wanted to help. I wouldn't be much of a man if I hadn't."

"Still, thank you. But I really do feel like I'm going to fall over, so I'm going to head home."

He didn't protest her leaving, instead accompanied her off the dance floor as the Teagues struck up another lively tune.

"I'll see you around," she said as she retrieved her purse from the bar stool where Ginny was sitting.

"You leaving already, sweetie?" Verona asked.

Liam didn't miss the meaningful glance his way. He almost laughed at the fact that Verona didn't even try to hide what she was thinking.

"Yeah, I'm beat."

"Well, at least let Liam walk you to your car. Can't be too careful nowadays."

India gave Verona a look that said she wondered if the older woman had lost her mind. "I don't think T.J. having a few too many has suddenly made Blue Falls a hotbed of crime."

"I don't mind," Liam said. The fact was, it would make him feel better to see her safely to her car.

Liam kept his hands to himself as he escorted India out of the building even though he really wanted to take her in his arms again. It hadn't seemed to matter that they were worlds different when they'd been dancing. He mentally scolded himself. Was he really going to let a single dance cloud his judgment?

When India reached her car and turned toward him, he thought the answer might be yes.

India took a deep breath, as if trying to get up the courage to say something. "I'm sorry about Verona. She can be a little—"

"Obvious?"

India lowered her gaze and fidgeted with her car keys. Without even trying she made him want to touch her.

"You caught that, huh?"

"Yeah, but you don't have to worry. We have a business relationship, a short-term one at that. Not wise to complicate things."

"Uh, right. That's what I've been telling them."

Was he imagining the sound of forced conviction in her words? Was it going to keep company with the bitter taste of his own? He'd said them to put at least a verbal barrier between them, to remind himself that he didn't need a complication like India in his life—no matter how pretty she was. No matter how much he was fighting the urge to back her against her car and kiss her senseless.

Before he did something stupid, he opened her door for her but kept it between them. "Be careful driving home."

"I will. It's not far. And thanks again, for everything."

As he watched India slip into her little car and drive away down the mostly deserted Main Street, he finally acknowledged to himself that keeping the relationship between them strictly professional was going to be easier said than done. She'd ensured that the moment she'd walked into the music hall wearing a red dress put on this earth for no other purpose than to fry every iota of common sense he'd ever possessed.

"Damn," he said. He was in trouble.

INDIA HAD ALWAYS BEEN A hard worker, but she kicked it up to an entirely new level the next day. She put out all the new stock she'd received, put a rack of items out on the sidewalk to draw in customers and completed everything on her rodeo list by noon. Well, everything she could do without talking with Liam about specifics to use in advertising the rodeo. And after she'd spent the first half of the day doing everything she could to avoid thinking about him and how it had felt to be held in his arms the night before, the last thing she needed to do was go see him.

So, she took the coward's way out and texted him, asking him to send her the details.

The front door opened and Keri Teague walked in with a white paper bag in one hand and a to-go coffee in the other.

"Did I place an order and forget it?" India asked.

"Nope, but you've seemed superbusy this morning, so I thought I'd bring you a snack. Apple pastry, fresh from the oven."

"I think I might love you."

"You sure it's me you're talking about?" Keri wore a grin that zapped India right back to the music hall the night before.

"Oh, no. Not you, too."

Keri held up her hands. "No, I'm not jumping on the Verona-Elissa matchmaking train. But I couldn't help but notice that the two of you look nice together."

"He'd look nice with anyone." Damn, had she said that out loud? "But he's not really my kind of guy."

"Okay, if you say so. I'm sure there are plenty of single ladies around town who will be glad to hear it. They certainly were giving him the eye last night."

India's teeth ground together at the idea, even though she had no right to feel that way. They'd agreed to keep things professional, after all. That's what she wanted, right?

"I'm glad you came over," India said, intent on changing the topic. She reached under the front counter and pulled out the folder containing the cupcake-contest entry forms. "I incorporated the list of rules you sent me so that it's all on one page."

Keri accepted the folder. "Great. I've already had people asking about it. I'm having trouble coming up with a third judge, though. I've got Marta Fleming," she said, referring to the president of the Blue Falls Bank. "She says she's way better at eating cupcakes than making them."

India smiled. "I'm right there with her on that."

"Good. I need people like you and Marta to keep me in business."

"True. So, let me guess. The second judge is Brooke."

"That's a no-brainer." Also true.

After all, Brooke was Keri's sister-in-law and the chef at the Teagues' guest ranch. India had heard nothing but wonderful praise about Brooke's cooking.

For some reason, the image of Ginny eating her bowl of ice cream at the music hall flitted through India's mind. "What about a kid as a third judge?"

"Hmm, interesting idea. Who'd you have in mind?"

"Ginny Parrish. I think she might enjoy it, and I think everyone else would get a kick out of her being a judge." She hoped Keri didn't read too much into her suggestion. It really wasn't more than trying to give Ginny something fun and a bit more girly to do while she was on location with her dad. She was a little tomboy, but India doubted even little tomboys could pass up tasting cupcakes.

"I like it. If she says yes, let me know and we'll have that part wrapped up."

India opened her mouth to suggest Keri ask Ginny, but what kind of sense did that make? Ginny didn't know Keri, and India already had to talk to Liam, anyway. This was just one more part of their professional relationship. "Okay."

"Well, I better get back to work before Sunshine marches over here and drags me back."

After Keri left, India checked her cell phone. Still no response from Liam. Didn't he know that she had a boatload to do and not a lot of time to do it in?

She didn't have time to focus on Liam or anything related to the rodeo, however, when her next customer entered the store.

"Good afternoon, Celene."

"It might be good if it were thirty degrees cooler."

India suppressed the not-so-nice comment that wanted to fly from her mouth. The one where she'd say something like, "If you don't like the heat, why did you leave Boston?"

In fact, Celene Bramwell came with her husband to Texas twenty years ago. But instead of going back to Massachusetts when he died, Celene had stayed. She continued to operate the high-end decor-and-furniture store farther down Main Street and play landlord to half a dozen residents in downtown Blue Falls, India included. Her favorite pastime was trying to turn Blue Falls into Boston's exclusive Newbery Street shopping district. She didn't seem to realize that most of the local residents wouldn't be able to shop in town if she succeeded. The clothing in India's store was one thing. A ten-thousand-dollar coffee table was quite another.

India shoved away her critical thoughts. After all, Celene wasn't just her landlord. She also was one of her best customers. "What can I do for you today, Celene?"

"I heard you had a new shipment."

"Indeed, I do." India motioned for Celene to precede her into the main display area. "There are some very nice tops and skirts that have a 1950s vibe. Also some flapper-inspired dresses and shoes."

India waited until Celene was deep into trying on clothes before she broached the topic of the empty space next door. "Have you thought any more about the vacancy?"

Celene handed India a pencil skirt with a slight flick of her hand that said she didn't want it. Then Celene's gaze shifted to the rest of the store. "I'm not sure expanding your store is a good business decision. It's not exactly over-crowded in here."

India's jaw tensed. It was all she could manage to not let her anger show. If she ever hoped to get access to that space, she had to stay on Celene's good side.

"I've done some mock-ups of how I could transform the space and be able to offer a lot more merchandise, cover different time periods. There are so many designers I love when I attend the trade shows, but I don't have enough room to adequately showcase everything I'd like to."

"Dreams and solid business decisions are not the same thing," Celene said. "Sometimes little, quaint and inconspicuous is quite enough."

Celene's choice of words irked India. Though on the surface Celene seemed to be talking about the store, India suspected there was more to it, that India shouldn't dare to dream too big, that she'd already accomplished more than anyone ever expected.

India turned away to return the discarded skirt to its hanger. She needed the extra moments to school her features. She wasn't going to give up on her plans for expansion, even though Verona's words from a few weeks before echoed in her head. Verona suspected that Celene was just stringing India along, making her think there was a chance she might eventually agree to lease her the space, when what she really wanted was a higher-dollar occupant, something she deemed more worthy.

When India faced Celene again, the older woman pointed at an outfit hanging on the wall. "I'll try that."

The moment Celene closed the door on the dressing room, India leaned her head against the cool metal of the circular clothing rack next to her. She didn't know whether to cry or scream. Of course, she did neither. Instead, she returned to the front of the store when she heard the ding of the door opening. She stopped short when she spotted Liam and Ginny standing there.

"Sorry I didn't text you back earlier, but I figured I could just give you all the details in person when we came to get some supplies at the hardware store."

India glanced over her shoulder to see if Celene needed anything. Why did Liam decide to stop by now of all times? Not that her heart didn't thump a little harder at the sight of him, but he'd obviously been working. Even Ginny was a bit smudged around the edges, and several strands of her hair were coming loose from her braid.

"Did I catch you at a bad time?" Liam asked.

India jerked her attention back to him, not wanting to be rude. "No, I'm sorry. I just have a customer trying on some things."

"We can come back."

India put out her hand to keep him from leaving. Who knew when she'd get the information she needed if she didn't nab it now. "Now is fine." She resisted looking over her shoulder again. Celene was used to having India's undivided attention when she came in to shop. "Have a seat." She ushered Liam and Ginny toward the table in the back.

Once they were seated, India perched on the edge of one of the chairs, ready to hurry to Celene's aid should the need arise.

Liam pushed a legal pad toward her. "I hope you can read my chicken scratch."

She had a difficult time even focusing on the words written on the page when he slid his forefinger down the edge of the paper. His hand was tanned and work-roughened, but she had the powerful urge to wrap her own around it. Reminding herself that she didn't need one more thing to worry about in her life, she forced herself to focus on the text.

"I've got everything you asked for," he said. "Names of the top riders who'll be here, the draws. The total prize amount, events, dates, times. You can add whatever extra activities you will be having in conjunction with the rodeo and information about who it all benefits."

"Dad said the girl has cancer," Ginny said. She sounded heartbroken for a girl she hadn't even met.

"She does, but that's why we're raising money for her, so she can get treatment and hopefully get better really soon."

"I want to be able to do something for her, too."

India's heart melted, and then she remembered her conversation with Keri. "As a matter of fact, I do have something you can do to help if you want to and your dad says it's okay."

"What?"

"India," Celene called out from the adjacent room, even though she could obviously see India was in the midst of a conversation.

After a momentary pressing together of her lips, India met Liam's eyes. "If you'll excuse me for a moment."

She went to attend to Celene, but she didn't rush as she might have any other day. Perhaps it was because she was tired, or maybe it had more to do with Celene's "advice" about enlarging the store, but India didn't feel like treating her like a queen today. "Can I help you with something else?"

Celene looked past India toward Liam. "Who is that man?" She wasn't quiet about it, either.

"Liam Parrish, the owner of the company putting on the benefit rodeo."

Celene didn't actually turn up her nose and sniff, but she might as well have. Probably not a lot of rodeos or hardworking cowboys in the Back Bay of Boston.

India was all for culture and nice things, but a person

didn't have to be a snob about it. Celene hadn't gotten that memo.

"You'd think he could have cleaned up a bit before he came into town." Thankfully, her words were a bit quieter this time.

India nearly laughed. It wasn't as if Liam was the first cowboy or ranch hand to stroll into town. After all, there was a hardware store on Main Street, and the Teagues owned one of the biggest ranches in the county.

Celene heaved a sigh then handed India the entire pile of clothes she'd just tried on.

"Would you like me to bag these up for you?"

"No. I'm going to Dallas tomorrow. I think I'll just wait and do my shopping there." Celene pulled her designer handbag onto her shoulder and started for the front door without even meeting India's eyes.

India stood in stunned silence for several moments, listening to the sound of Celene's heels on the wooden floor as she walked right past Liam and Ginny without even acknowledging them. Embarrassment flooded India that someone in Blue Falls would treat them so rudely.

Not wanting to deal with Celene's cast-offs, she tossed the pile of clothes onto the glass-topped table in front of the white chairs. When she turned and approached the front, Liam gave her a raised-eyebrow look. "Interesting lady," he said with a look toward the door.

She could tell exactly what he thought of Celene, but she admired how he didn't bad-mouth her in front of Ginny.

"And my landlord."

"Lucky you."

"She wasn't friendly," Ginny said.

Liam and India looked at each other and burst out laughing.

India slid onto her chair and squeezed Ginny's little

hand. "You are right about that. Must come with owning half of downtown, but enough about her. Where was I?"

"You were telling me how I could help Mia."

"Yes." India pointed out the front window toward Keri's store. "You see that bakery over there?"

Ginny half stood and craned her neck. "Yes."

"My friend Keri owns it, and she's having a cupcake contest during the rodeo. We were wondering if you'd like to be one of the three judges? You would get to taste each of the cupcakes people enter in the contest and vote for the ones you like the best."

Ginny's eyes widened, as did her smile as she looked at Liam. "Could I?"

"Hmm. Do I want my daughter hopped up on so much sugar she'll be bouncing all night?"

"Please, Dad," Ginny pleaded in that way that only little kids had mastered.

With a glance at India, Liam nodded. "Fine. But no sweets for a week after that or you'll have a mouth full of cavities."

"Deal."

India laughed when Ginny stuck out her hand across the table to shake hands with her dad, sealing the cupcake deal.

"Well, there's at least one thing I can mark off my to-do list."

"Speaking of to-do lists," Liam said as he stood. "We have some paint to go buy."

"How are things going?" India asked the question partly because she wanted to know, but she had to admit that there was a little part of her that wanted Liam to stay a bit longer. That was a desire she was going to have to do something to quell. Maybe *GQ* would come to town to do a shoot of sexy, successful businessmen, and she'd be saved from herself.

"Good. We should be able to wrap up work on the barn

today. Then it's on to the grandstands and prepping the inside of the arena. We could always use an extra pair of hands if you decide to get some fresh air."

India nearly snorted. "I'm pretty sure I'd be the world's worst handyman...handyperson...whatever."

"You might be right about that." Liam grinned then turned his attention to where Ginny had wandered up to the jewelry counter and nearly had her nose pressed against the glass. "You ready to go, kiddo?"

Ginny stepped quickly away from the display case, almost as if she'd been caught doing something wrong. "Yep."

After India waved goodbye to them and they headed down the sidewalk, she crossed to where Ginny had been standing and looked in the case. She wondered what item inside had attracted the little girl's attention and if her dad had even noticed.

From everything India had seen, Liam was as good a dad as he could be to Ginny. But he was still a guy, and guys weren't what one would call observant sometimes, especially when it came to what women wanted. And while Ginny was a long way from being a woman, she was still female. India wondered if underneath the minicowgirl trying to emulate her father beat the heart of a little girl wanting something pretty.

It was India who jumped away from the case this time when the front door opened. Liam stood half in and half out of the door.

"Sorry, quick question. Your friend with the bakery, does she do birthday cakes?"

India nodded. "Yes, she's a master with cakes."

"Good, thanks." He started to leave.

"Wait. Why?"

"Oh, Ginny's birthday is right before the rodeo. I thought

since she'd be here instead of at home that I'd at least get her a cake."

Maybe Ginny wouldn't mind hanging out with a bunch of rodeo cowboys and cowgirls on her birthday, but it didn't sit well with India. It was as if the past grabbed her and yanked her back to all the birthdays she'd spent with parents who either forgot about her big day or gave her a half-hearted celebration before they either drank themselves into oblivion or got so high they forgot who she was.

"How about I order it for you?"

His forehead creased. "I can order a cake."

"I know, but I have to go see Keri, anyway. And I'm familiar with all the different kinds of cakes she can make."

He seemed to be thinking about her offer, and she hoped she wasn't overstepping. "Okay, just let me know how much it is, and I'll swing by the bakery to pay for it."

India nodded, already thinking about all the possibilities. But what was Ginny interested in? Maybe she could devise a way to find out between now and then.

And for the second time in as many minutes, Liam left her alone in her store. After taking a deep breath, she looked toward the pile of discarded clothes. Was Celene right? Would expanding the store be a mistake? She let the lack of customers worry her, a lull that normally wouldn't have registered. But Celene had put the doubt in her mind, and now India wondered if Blue Falls was big enough to fulfill her dreams.

Chapter Six

Liam shook hands with James Humphreys, who'd be providing several of the bulls and a couple of broncs for the upcoming rodeo. "Sounds like a deal to me."

"So, you going to be riding in this one?"

Liam swept off his hat and wiped sweat from his forehead. "Hadn't really thought about it. Been too busy pulling everything else together."

"Remember, it's use it or lose it." With that, James waved and headed for his truck.

As James drove away from the fairgrounds, Liam spotted India's car followed by a blue pickup truck that had a few years and dents on it. Damn if his pulse didn't kick up a notch. With a shake of his head, he sauntered toward the vehicles. When a guy stepped out and smiled at India as he rounded the front of his truck, a surge of unexpected jealousy shot through Liam. What the hell? They'd agreed to stick to a professional relationship. And good thing since they were nothing alike and after the rodeo would probably never see each other again. Fort Worth to Blue Falls was a bit of a drive to pick up a date.

So why did he feel this overwhelming urge to step between her and this guy and sweep her into his arms?

He needed to go out on a date, just not with froufrou India Pike.

She spotted Liam then and waved. He nodded as she turned toward the passenger door of the truck. A little girl who looked to be about Ginny's age, but paler and thinner, opened the door and slipped out as the guy hovered.

It suddenly dawned on Liam who this must be as he crossed the distance between him and the others.

"Hey, Liam," India said. "Is Ginny around?"

"She's in the barn playing with a cat that took up residence overnight."

India glanced toward the barn. "I thought she might like to meet Mia." She shifted her attention to the man standing with his hand on Mia's shoulder. "This is Jake Monroe, Mia's father."

Liam shook the other man's hand. "Good to meet you."

"You, too. We appreciate all you're doing here."

"Just doing my job, and glad to help." Liam shifted his attention to Mia and bent to her level. He extended his hand to her the same way he had her father. "And, Mia, it's very nice to meet you."

Mia gave him a shy look before putting her small hand in his. "Are you a real rodeo cowboy?"

He smiled. "Yes, I am."

"She's been asking a million questions about the rodeo ever since she found out about it," Jake said.

"Well, then. I should give you the grand tour." Liam extended his arm.

Mia giggled as she wrapped her fingers around his arm.

Liam glanced toward India, and she gave him a smile that made his heart swell. He smiled back then turned all of his attention on Mia as he guided her to the arena, telling her about all the different events that would be included in the rodeo.

"And India and her friends are planning a lot of other

activities, too. They even roped my little girl into being a judge in a cupcake contest."

The bright look on Mia's face dimmed a little. "I wish there was something I could do."

Her words and the reason behind them broke his heart. He didn't know how Jake Monroe was able to get through the day knowing his little girl was fighting for her life. But he guessed Jake had no choice. He had to be strong enough for both of them.

As they turned for the barn, Liam's mind searched for some way Mia could contribute without overtaxing her. He hit on it just as they entered the barn. "You know, I do have something you could do."

"Really?" Mia sounded so hopeful he wanted to scoop her up and hold her close, add another layer of protection to her father's.

"Yes. Every rodeo needs a rodeo queen, and we don't have one. Do you think you'd be interested in something like that?"

"Yes!" She paused for a moment. "What does a rodeo queen do?"

Everyone laughed, and Jake ruffled his daughter's sandy hair. "Maybe you should ask that before you agree, squirt."

"Oh, it's a very important job," Liam said. "You would ride in at the beginning of the rodeo, leading in all the riders who would be competing. That is, if your dad says it's okay." He probably should have asked Jake first, but the offer had just slipped out.

Mia, showing more energy than she had since arriving, looked up at her dad with a pleading expression on her face. "Oh, please, Daddy, can I?"

"You can ride in with her," Liam said, trying to put her father at ease.

"If you feel okay, then sure."

Mia hugged her dad, seemingly with all the strength she could muster.

"And I think I can help with a little something to wear," India said.

"You don't have to do that," Jake said.

India waved away his concern. "It would be my honor. After all, it's not every day that Blue Falls has a queen in town."

That settled, Liam motioned for them to follow him the rest of the way into the barn. "Ginny?"

Ginny popped up from one of the far stalls, an orange cat in her arms.

Liam waved her out. "India brought someone for you to meet."

Ginny stepped out of the stall and set the cat down next to her feet. The cat seemed to be just as attached to her as she was to it since it stuck close as she approached.

"This is Mia," Liam said. "Mia, my daughter, Ginny, and her new best friend."

"Peach."

Liam laughed a little and shook his head. "Honey, you know that cat may live around here somewhere and probably already has a name."

"No, he doesn't have a collar."

He opened his mouth to tell her that didn't mean he didn't have an owner, but then he noticed Mia bent down and rubbed the cat's head. The cat really was good-natured and seemed to enjoy the attention.

"I like the name Peach," Mia said.

It really did fit considering his coloring. They could have the cat conversation later, if the cat was still around in a few days.

With the girls occupied, the adults wandered to the opposite end of the barn.

"I appreciate what you did for her." Jake sounded genuinely appreciative but also bone-deep tired.

"It's good for everyone," Liam said.

Jake's phone buzzed, and he pulled it out to check the text message. He glanced at Mia then back at the phone. "I hate to pull her away, but we've got to go. Bill's got an extra delivery run for me."

India looked toward where the girls were giggling and getting along as if they were already the best of friends. "Why don't you let her stay with me until you get back? Once we're done here, I can take her back to the shop. She can play dress-up for a while."

"I couldn't ask you to do that."

"You didn't ask me. I offered. Really, it's no problem at all. We might even wander down to the Primrose for a slice of pie."

"I'm never going to be able to repay you," Jake said.

"Don't be silly. Seeing Mia get better will be payment enough."

Jake pulled India into his arms for a hug then a peck on the cheek. A flash of jealousy hit Liam again, but it was gone the moment Jake let go of India and headed into the barn to tell Mia about the change of plans. For India's part, she looked a little startled, but her heart was also sitting out on her sleeve as she watched Mia hug her dad goodbye.

"That was a nice thing to do for him," Liam said.

India shifted her gaze to Liam. "He needs the work. Jake has a small ranch, but he also drives a delivery truck for one of the local flower growers. Bill, his boss, is trying to give him as many extra deliveries as he can when Jake is able to be away from Mia."

"He's a single parent?"

India nodded and turned a little toward Liam. "This is extra hard on him because Mia's mom died of cancer when

Mia was only two. Different kind, but still it was a huge shock when Mia was diagnosed."

Liam fought a sudden lump in his throat. He thought he'd been thrown a lot of curveballs in his life. It was nothing next to Jake Monroe's challenges. "Some people just get the crap end of the stick in life."

"Yeah. But he's been really good at trying to keep her spirits up. And speaking of doing good things, that was a great idea about the rodeo queen."

He shrugged. "It was nothing."

India touched his arm. "It wasn't nothing. You made that little girl's day, probably her month."

Why did the mere feel of her hand on his arm make his body go warm all over, a warmth that had nothing to do with the heat of the day? He wondered if she saw his thoughts in his eyes when he looked at her because she moved her hand back down to her side and shifted her gaze to where the girls were deep in conversation, as if they'd known each other their entire lives.

"Do you mind if Ginny comes with Mia?"

"To your store?"

"Yes. I think they might enjoy spending the day together."

"Ginny's not really girly."

"You might be surprised."

Liam looked at India, searching for censure in her expression, but saw none. But what was she really thinking? That he didn't know his daughter as well as he thought he did? That rubbed him the wrong way, but a little part of him wondered if she could possibly be right.

India laughed as Ginny tried on a blue pillbox hat and struck a pose. Ginny joined in the laughter as Mia clunked across the floor in a pair of heels about twice the size of her feet.

"I think you both have a future in modeling," India said.

One of the two customers browsing the store smiled at the girls' antics. "If you added a children's section, I think it'd be a big hit."

In all her plans for expansion, she'd never considered adding children's wear. But now the idea took root, and her imagination was off and running. Maybe the store could even host dress-up parties as an extra service for mothers wanting to shop for their own clothing.

"There was a fashion show here today and we weren't invited?"

India glanced away from the girls at the sound of Elissa's voice. Skyler stood to her side. "Oh, I forgot about our meeting."

"Evidently. But I can multitask." Elissa stepped past India and plunked down in one of the cushy white chairs while Skyler rounded the table to sit in another.

Before she joined her friends, India turned to her customers. "Can I help you ladies with anything?"

One left without buying anything, but India followed the other to the cash register for a nice-size sale. Take that, Celene Bramwell.

When she returned to the other room, Skyler and Elissa were laughing at the girls' continued antics.

"Did Mia tell you all she is going to be the rodeo queen?"

"Oh, that's impressive," Skyler said.

Mia beamed.

"So, Ginny, you've been to lots of rodeos. What does a rodeo queen wear?" India asked.

"Jeans, shirt, hat, boots."

Well, that didn't sound very queenly. India made a mental note to do some online searching later, then find the best little rodeo queen outfit she could for Mia.

As the girls continued to play, making up little stories to go along with their accessories, India turned to her friends. "Sorry for the delay. We should get to work now."

"So when did you become a babysitter?" Elissa asked.

"It's just an afternoon, so Jake could get an extra run to Austin in."

"And Ginny?"

India knew by the look on her friend's face that she was really asking what this meant about her and Liam. In truth, she couldn't think too much about seeing Liam again because the man still gave her a jittery, buzzy feeling every time she was near him.

"I thought they could keep each other entertained while I worked."

"Uh-huh." Elissa didn't sound convinced that was all there was to the story.

India pretended that she didn't notice and pulled out her notes regarding the rodeo. They all went over everything they'd finished and where they stood on all the other projects.

"Are you going to have funnel cake?" Ginny asked.

"Would you like there to be?" Skyler asked.

"Yes!" Both girls answered with great enthusiasm at the same time.

Skyler made a note on her list. "Funnel cake it is."

By the time India, Elissa and Skyler wrapped things up, Mia looked a bit more tired than she should have. That sent a shot of fear through India. Had she allowed Mia to do too much?

"Girls, why don't I let you watch some cartoons?" She led them to her office, where she had a small TV on her desk and a love seat in one corner. She turned the TV toward them before grabbing her laptop and returning to the front of the store.

"I think you might make a good mom someday," Elissa said.

"Don't be silly. Babysitting for one afternoon doesn't make me mom material."

"But you're always really good with the girls in the Blue-Belles classes, too," Skyler added.

"A little 'cart before the horse,' aren't we?"

"I don't think you'd have to look too hard to find the horse," Elissa said with a bump of her shoulder to India's.

Even after her friends left, India couldn't shift her focus to work. She found herself either checking on the girls or staring out the window thinking about Liam, about how simply touching his arm earlier had made her tingle all over and grow breathless.

Though it probably wasn't the best idea in the world, she did a search for Liam's name and hit upon some photos from rodeos. She'd never been one to go for cowboys, at least that's what she'd told herself, but she couldn't help how her heart sped up at the look of him in tight jeans, chaps and that ever-present hat. The man looked like hot sex on two long legs.

Why did she have to keep reminding herself that he wasn't the type of man with whom she wanted to spend her life?

Trying to shift her attention elsewhere, she forced herself to do some online searches for rodeo queens, checking out their attire to see how she might adapt it for Mia. She was in the midst of checking some online catalogs when Jake walked in the front door.

"How's she doing?" he asked.

"Good. They played dress-up for a while, but they're watching cartoons now." India slid off her stool and headed for her office. When she stepped inside the office, she found the girls leaning against each other fast asleep. "Well, looks like they decided it was nap time."

Jake came to stand behind her. "Thank you."

"It was nothing," she said, echoing Liam's earlier words.

"No, this was good, for both of us. Her color is better now than it's been in several days."

India let out a breath she hadn't been fully aware she was holding. "Oh, good. I was so afraid I'd let her do too much."

"I try to let her do as much as she can. I don't want her to feel like an invalid. If I treat her like everything is normal, hopefully she won't be as scared."

"You're a good father, Jake."

"And you're a really good friend. Thank you." Jake moved past her and scooped Mia into his arms. This woke both girls, who said their sleepy goodbyes.

Once they were gone, India was suddenly left with only the daughter of the man she'd been daydreaming about moments before.

"You want to watch more cartoons?"

Ginny stretched and shook her head. "You said we could get pie."

India smiled. A girl after her own heart. But as they headed for the front door, India glanced across the street. "I have a better idea."

She set the be back in sign for ten minutes and locked the door behind them. As they crossed the street, she was careful to hold Ginny's hand.

The front of the Mehlerhaus Bakery was empty when they stepped inside.

"Be with you in a minute," Keri called out from somewhere out of sight. A few seconds passed before she hurried out of her office, smoothing her hair.

India got a good idea why when Sheriff Simon Teague,

Keri's new husband, followed her with a mischievous grin on his face. India didn't have to see Keri's cheeks to know that they were probably blazing, and that Simon probably found that quite humorous. The sexual tension in the room was as thick as fog, and India shifted from one foot to the other, suddenly feeling edgy and…needy.

Out of nowhere, India imagined Liam pulling her into a hiding place and stealing kisses. Now Keri wasn't the only one with an extra flush of blood warming her face.

As Simon headed for the door, he tapped the brim of his Stetson with his forefinger. "Good afternoon, India." He smiled at Ginny. "Ma'am."

Ginny giggled as Simon headed out the front door, back to protecting the good folks of Blue Falls.

"How can I help you two?" Keri approached the glass display in the front of the bakery, racks filled with doughnuts, pastries and cakes.

"I thought you might like to meet your third cupcake judge." India placed her hand on Ginny's back and tried not to think about how easy and natural it felt. "This is Ginny Parrish."

"So you're my lifesaver," Keri said. "I think that deserves a treat." Keri pointed at the display case. "Pick whatever you'd like, Ginny."

While Ginny examined the choices, India went to stand across from Keri. "I see the newlywed shine hasn't dulled any."

"The man is impossible. I'm going to have to bar him from the bakery so I can get my work done."

India smiled, genuinely happy for Keri's happiness. She'd been through a lot, losing most of her family and being thrust into being a mom for her orphaned niece. But she'd finally found her Mr. Right, and he'd been under her nose the entire time. Again, India's thoughts went to Liam.

No matter how hard she tried, she couldn't stop thinking about him, about what it might feel like to let go and explore what at least part of her was wanting.

"India?"

"What? I'm sorry."

"I asked if you wanted something, too."

Yeah, a tall cowboy who refused to vacate her thoughts. "No, I'm good."

"So how'd you end up playing babysitter?"

India told her about how it had come about then tried to pay for the lemon cupcake with a bumblebee on top that Ginny chose.

"No, consider this a thank-you for finding my third judge. And Ginny, come back anytime. And bring your dad and India with you."

"I will," Ginny said then started for the door.

India met Keri's eyes, wondering why it seemed the entire town seemed to be on the "fix up India with Liam" bandwagon.

Keri shrugged. "Sorry, Verona got to me."

India shook her head and followed Ginny, thinking she needed to find a date, an appropriate one, so everyone would back off.

Again, she held Ginny's hand as they crossed the street. When she looked up the sidewalk and noticed Celene standing outside the front door of Yesterwear, and not looking too happy about it, India stifled a curse. Just what she needed right now.

"Celene," she said in as friendly a voice as she could as they drew near. "Good to see you."

Celene spared a quick glance at Ginny before focusing her disapproving eyes on India. "It really isn't good for business to not have reliable hours."

"We just stepped across the street for a moment to get

a snack. Sorry to keep you waiting." India cringed as she figured this was another strike against her in Celene's eyes. She pushed her concerns down as she unlocked the door and let Celene in.

Celene stopped at the front counter and pulled out her wallet. "Get me that beige lace top I tried on."

India gritted her teeth as she went to do Celene's bidding. Why couldn't the woman say please and thank you every now and then?

Who was she kidding? She knew why. Celene Bramwell considered herself several rungs higher on the social ladder than everyone in Blue Falls, so many rungs above India that they couldn't even see each other. But she was a substantial property holder and not so dreadful that anyone told her to kiss their behinds.

India pressed her lips together to keep from laughing at the image of doing exactly that.

When she returned to the front with the blouse, Celene made quick work of paying and leaving.

"Is she mad?" Ginny asked.

"No, honey. I think she's just in a hurry." And a snob, but she didn't say that.

When Liam stepped in the front door, India immediately worried that he would be able to tell she'd been searching for pictures of him.

"Your best buddy just blew by me like she was trying to escape a fire," he said.

"Busy lady," India said, thinking a whole lot more.

"She's not nice to India," Ginny said.

India smoothed the top of Ginny's hair. "It's okay. I'm used to it." She shouldn't have said that out loud, but it had slipped out, frustration leaking through the cracks Celene seemed to expose in her.

"That doesn't make it right," Liam said.

The edge in his voice, the way he leaped to her defense, made India fall for him a little. When she allowed herself to meet his gaze, she thought it might be more than a little.

Chapter Seven

Liam fought the urge to do harm. He would never actually hurt a woman, but he sure could tell one to learn some manners. He'd start with the woman who'd hurt India's feelings. India acted as if it was no big deal, that it was just part of a life in retail, but he didn't think that was the entire story. For a moment, he'd seen the deep hurt in her eyes that had been there the night the drunk guy had manhandled her at the music hall. He'd not been close enough to hear what he'd said to her, but it had cut.

It looked as if there were more layers to India Pike than superficial materialism. There was also sympathy and kindness toward a sick little girl and her father. A close and teasing relationship with her two friends. The caring that led her to include Ginny in the festivities she was planning.

And then there was something deeper she tried to hide. Pain. He wasn't sure how he knew that based on only a couple of quick glimpses, but he did. And despite the fact that he barely knew her, he found himself wanting to make that pain go away.

But that wasn't his task to undertake, was it?

He noticed that she looked uncomfortable with him watching her, so he shifted his attention to Ginny. "Did you have a good time today?"

"Yeah. We played dress-up and watched cartoons. When

Mia left, India took me to the bakery and I had a bumble-bee cupcake. It was so cute."

"Well, that does sound like a good afternoon. Maybe I should make you work tomorrow, and I'll come have a cupcake."

Ginny giggled, a sound that always made his heart swell.

When he looked at India again, she was back to the person he'd met that first day—stylish shopkeeper with no hint of what lay beneath.

"Thanks for letting Ginny hang out here this afternoon."

"We had a good time. Your daughter is quite the little model."

"Really?" He didn't like not knowing something about his own daughter.

"Yes, she and Mia were entertaining anyone who came into the store."

"She's got lots of pretty stuff," Ginny said.

Was it his imagination, or did Ginny sound like a different kid all of a sudden? A stab of fear hit him, that if he let this continue she might turn out to be more like her mother. He didn't think he could stand watching his kindhearted little tomboy turn into someone like Charlotte, more concerned with how she looked and her own wants than anyone else's. Selfish, spoiled, willing to walk over anyone to get what she wanted.

"We've taken up enough of India's time," he said as he motioned for Ginny to head for the door. "Time to go back to the real world."

For a moment, he thought Ginny might argue. But she must have thought better of it. Still, he couldn't help but notice how she dragged her feet.

Then he made the mistake of meeting India's eyes. The hurt look was back. He cursed himself because this time he knew he was the one who put it there.

INDIA HELD HERSELF TOGETHER until Liam and Ginny left. He'd probably meant nothing by it other than Ginny's playtime was over, but his words about how they were heading back to the real word had hurt. She couldn't even put her finger on why. Did he think that her shop and the beautiful things in it didn't matter? Did he want to remind Ginny that rodeos and cowboys and getting dirty were the real world to him?

Maybe he hadn't meant it that way, but it felt like a slap to everything she was, everything she'd worked hard to build for herself.

She sank onto the stool, more tired than she should have been. Thank goodness it was only a few minutes until closing time. Even though she owned her own business and could leave whenever she wanted, Celene's words banged around in her head, making her paranoid about leaving. It wasn't as if Celene were sitting outside watching her every move, but it certainly felt like it.

To pass the time, she did some more online searching until she found the perfect little cowgirl outfit for Mia—a pink, Western-style shirt with white fringe, pink boots and white chaps. To top it all off, literally, a white hat that had little rhinestones affixed to the front to look like a tiara. It was perfect—one part cowgirl, one part princess.

The site had a lot more adorable outfits, and darned if she didn't find herself buying another little pair of boots. This pair was red with little brown horses stitched into the leather. She was probably a fool for buying them for Ginny. After all, she really didn't know Ginny. And Liam might very well want to keep it that way.

Maybe she should have drawn the line on getting involved in her birthday by arranging for Keri to make a cake, which she still needed to do.

Looking up at the clock, she noticed it was two minutes

past her official closing time, safe to leave. She powered down the computer, slipped it into her bag, prepared her bank deposit and headed out the door.

"Oh, good. I'm glad I caught you, dear," Verona said as she hurried down the sidewalk.

If this was another matchmaking attempt, India was going to run the opposite direction. "What's up?"

"I just made a big batch of barbecue, and I need people to help me eat it. Elissa and Skyler are coming over. Pete's been over cleaning out my gutters, so I even convinced him to stay."

"Sounds like you've got several mouths to feed already, so I'm going to pass. I'm so tired, all I want to do is go home and collapse on my couch."

"I think you vastly underestimate how much barbecue I made."

In Texas, barbecue typically meant beef. But since Verona's vacation to Memphis a few years ago, she'd been all about pulled pork barbecue.

"You're not going to let me take a rain check, are you?"

"Nope," Verona said as she wrapped her arm around India's. "Think of it this way. If you eat now, you won't have to cook when you go home."

India hadn't planned on it. A phone call to Gino's for pizza delivery had been much more likely.

"Okay, fine. I'll stay long enough to eat one sandwich, and then I've got a date with a nice, long soak in the tub and then my pajamas."

"Deal."

There was a little too much victory in Verona's voice for India to be comfortable. She didn't breathe easily until she got to Verona's and saw that the only people filling the backyard were the ones she'd mentioned.

It wasn't until she'd taken the first bite of her barbecue

sandwich that she looked up to see two new arrivals—
Liam and Ginny.

"I am going to kill that old woman yet," India muttered
under her breath. She met Elissa's eyes across the table.
"Did you have anything to do with this?"

Elissa put up her hands, palms out. "This time, no. On
my honor."

Ginny ran up to India. "I didn't know you would be
here."

India spotted Liam stepping up behind his daughter. "I
didn't, either, until a few minutes ago," she said.

"Let's go get some barbecue, squirt," Liam said as he
pointed Ginny toward the table with the food.

India stared after them for a moment. Did Liam believe
her that she'd had no idea they were coming here? Suddenly
fed up with the day and how she was letting everyone else's
opinions trump her own, India stood.

"Are you leaving?" Elissa asked.

"Yes." Without giving an explanation, she tossed her
barely touched sandwich in the trash can and made her way
around the side of the house toward the driveway.

But when she reached her car, she spotted the flat tire
on the back of the driver's side. "You have got to be kidding me." She felt like kicking it, but all that would achieve
would be ruining another pair of nice shoes and quite possibly breaking her toe.

"Need some help?"

India wanted to just start walking, then foist this whole
rodeo off on Verona. Of course, she did neither. Instead,
she turned slowly toward Liam. He'd showered since she'd
seen him earlier, and damn if he didn't look even sexier
in clean jeans, a worn T-shirt and still-damp hair. It took
a monumental effort not to walk toward him and run her

fingers through it. As it was, she might have licked her lips. She wasn't sure.

"I'm wondering if that little old lady has enough strength to shank my tire."

Liam laughed. "I wouldn't put it past her."

"I'm sorry about this," India said. "I'll talk with her to-morrow."

He waved off her concern, which seemed to be a total turnaround from how he'd acted only a couple of minutes before when he'd spotted her in the backyard. He pointed toward the rear of her car. "You have a spare?"

"Yeah, one of those little doughnut things."

He headed past her. "Pop the trunk."

"You don't have to do this. I can call Greg over at the garage."

"I can have this done before he can even get here."

India turned to follow him as he headed for the trunk. "You do realize he could be here in like five minutes tops, right?"

He grinned at her. "So I'm fast."

She snorted and popped the trunk.

Liam pulled out the tire and the jack then set to work lifting the car. "Does Verona hound your friends as much as she does you?"

"She's been known to more than gently nudge them from time to time, but I seem to be this month's lucky winner of her undivided attention."

Liam's biceps bulged as he twisted the lug nuts on the flat tire. India swallowed at the sight before forcing herself to look away down the street that ended at the southern end of Main.

True to his word, Liam made quick work of the change. He had the flat tire off, the new one on and everything back in the trunk before she could think about how to make their current situation not so awkward.

He closed the trunk and dusted off his hands. "You think she'd give up if we actually went out?"

India jerked her gaze to his, unsure she'd heard him correctly. "What?"

"You know, play along. Maybe if we actually went out a time or two, then you could tell her you tried and that it didn't work out. End of problem."

India didn't like how her insides twisted at the thought that he might think of them going out as a problem. But then she remembered that was exactly what it would be. They were business associates, acquaintances, nothing more. She feared even pretending to date might endanger that. She might not ever admit it to anyone else, but she was intensely attracted to Liam despite the fact he had absolutely nothing in common with the type of guy she'd always maintained she wanted. But the reality was that her blood raced every time she was around him. Could she pretend to be on a date with him without caving in and making it real?

"That would probably just add fuel to the fire."

Liam looked up the driveway toward the backyard. "You know her better than I do, so I'll take your word for it. If you change your mind, though, let me know."

She couldn't help fidgeting under his gaze. What exactly did he mean by that? He couldn't actually want to go out with her, could he?

When he finally broke eye contact and headed back up the driveway, she was able to take a deep breath. He'd taken a few steps when she remembered what he'd just done for her.

"Thanks for the help."

"No problem."

A few more steps and he was gone, leaving India stand-

ing in the driveway imagining her feet stuck in concrete so
she wouldn't run after him and take him up on his offer.

SOMEHOW INDIA MANAGED to finally fall asleep, helped by
the long bath she'd taken the moment she got home. Her
state of mind hadn't been helped by imagining Liam in the
bathtub with her. But there seemed to be no stopping those
kinds of thoughts from strolling through her head no matter how much she tried. Finally, she'd given in and let her
imagination run free. That had resulted in some very nice
dreams. She had no idea how she was going to face Liam
the next time they had to see each other without her face
going up in flames.

Despite everything, she had a really good morning. She
was busy enough with a steady flow of customers that she
didn't have a lot of time to fantasize about a guy who would
not only be out of her life, but also hours away before the
calendar turned to July.

The amount of sales encouraged her to pull out her plans
for the building next door. She wasn't going to give up trying to convince Celene that the right use for the space was
an expansion of Yesterwear. She wanted to make her store a
hub of destination shopping. More than once she'd imagined
people driving from Austin and San Antonio just to be able
to buy clothing from her carefully selected merchandise.

When she looked at the plans, she erased some of what
she'd drawn on the sketch pad and rearranged previous
ideas. Where she'd had an area devoted to vintage coats,
she drew a quarter circle in one corner for a stage and a
set of three changing rooms next to it and a semicircle of
couches facing the stage. She smiled when she imagined a
parade of little girls trying on vintage-inspired outfits just
their size. Maybe she could even work with Keri to cater
the parties.

She got so excited about the new ideas that she couldn't get them down on paper fast enough. She almost resented when the front door opened again. When she looked up and saw Skyler, she relaxed.

"Hey, come here," India said, waving her friend toward the front counter. "I've got a lot of new ideas for the space next door."

"Did you get Celene to approve the expansion?"

"Not yet, but I'm not giving up."

"Then what's going on over there?"

"What?"

Skyler gestured in the direction of the vacant store. "The front door is open and Justine is in there showing around a couple of guys."

"What?" India realized she'd just uttered the same one-word question twice then shook her head. "Can you watch the store a minute?"

"Sure."

India hurried next door. When she stepped inside, she spotted Justine Ware, who owned the real estate company a couple more doors down the street. With her were two men in suits. One of them turned at her entrance, catching India off guard with his impeccable good looks. At a glance, she knew his suit cost more than her family had often had to buy groceries for six months. On the outside, he looked like her fantasy guy. But because of where he stood right now, she was afraid he was more of a threat than a potential mate.

"Hey, India," Justine said.

"What's going on here?"

Justine looked a little startled by her tone and excused herself from the men. As Justine walked toward India, the younger of the two men, the one in the stylish suit, smiled at India. Of course he had perfect teeth. She'd bet he had a sports car and quite possibly had traveled to at least three foreign countries, too.

"Is something wrong?" Justine asked as she drew close. "Who are those guys?"

"Real estate developers from San Marcos."

"Why are they in here?"

Justine's forehead crinkled. "They're considering buying the space."

"But it's not for sale." India's heart grew heavy because she already knew what Justine was going to say next.

"Celene listed it late yesterday."

India fought tears and struggled to take a steadying breath. "Why would she do that? She knew I wanted to lease the space."

"Oh, I'm sorry." Justine looked genuinely regretful to be the bearer of bad news. "I didn't know."

"It's not your fault." India's words came out in a half-choked whisper. Not able to even look at the space that had been the centerpiece of her dream for so long, she turned on her heel and rushed back out onto the sidewalk. She leaned against the side of the building, trying not to think about all her plans falling in a pile of ashes around her.

Why had Celene decided to sell, and so soon after they'd talked about India leasing the space? It had either been a sudden decision, or she'd simply not had the decency to tell India her plans. Either way, it ticked her off. If she'd had plans to sell all along, Celene could have at least given India first dibs.

But Celene knew India didn't have that kind of money. Never had, and from Celene's point of view never would. Something ugly squirmed inside India. She'd likely never be able to prove it, but India suspected that Celene's decision had a lot more to do with India's past than her present or future. And here India had thought most people had let it go, had allowed her to distinguish herself as more than her genetics. But T.J.'s outburst at the music hall and now this…well, she wondered if she'd been deluding herself all along. Had she made a mistake by not leaving Blue Falls for good?

She shook her head. No, her best friends were here. The vast majority of the residents were wonderful people who always greeted her with a smile.

But could they look at her and not see who she'd once been? Who her parents had been? What her parents had done?

She wanted to believe she was overthinking, reading too much into recent events. But once tempted out into the light of day, those old doubts dug in their claws.

The sound of approaching steps along with the sudden realization that she was drawing a couple of curious stares prompted India back to her store. When she walked through the front door, Skyler hopped up from the stool behind the front counter.

"Are you okay?" Skyler rounded the jewelry case, concern etched on her face.

"Celene put the building up for sale."

"Without telling you?"

India nodded.

"When?"

"Last night."

"And there are already people looking? That's surprising, especially since I didn't recognize them."

Meaning they were from out of town. Would they buy it? And what did they want it for?

The door opened behind India, drawing her attention. She hid her feelings as she turned, ready to help a customer. But it was Justine and the two men. Justine gave her an apologetic look.

"Can I help you all?" India smiled. After all, if these men would be her new neighbors, best to be friendly.

The younger of the two, he of the slick suit, smiled and extended his hand. "Hello. You ran off before we could introduce ourselves. I'm Kevin Sladen, and this is my business partner, Mark Raybourn."

India shook his hand, noting the firm grip and the way he held her hand a little longer than necessary. The hint of mischief in his blue eyes added to his physical appeal, but she was too upset to respond to it the way he was probably used to. As she released her grip and shook hands with his partner, she remembered to respond. "Nice to meet you both."

"We'll try not to get in your way," Mark said as he glanced past her.

India looked from him to Kevin and finally to Justine. "I don't understand."

Justine looked as if she wanted to crawl into a hole. "Celene is selling this building, too."

Chapter Eight

India just stared at Justine, hoping she hadn't heard her correctly. "Excuse me?"

"No need to worry," Kevin said, drawing her attention back to him. "We're just looking now. If we decide to buy, we may only need the building next door. Depends on if we land a couple of big projects we're bidding on."

India felt as if she'd been dropped in the middle of some country where she didn't speak the language. She shook her head, as if that might clear the confusion.

"Mr. Sladen and Mr. Raybourn are architects."

"We're looking for a place to expand into the Hill Country. The space next door will be sufficient if it's just us, but we have a partnership with a builder who may want to expand with us and will need the extra space."

"You do realize this space is already occupied?" Bless Skyler for voicing India's thoughts, the ones caught up in the maelstrom of emotions and questions whirling inside her.

To their credit, the two men suddenly looked uncomfortable.

"Like we said, it might not work out," Mark muttered.

"We'd still like to take a quick look around, if that's okay with you," Kevin said, giving her what she suspected was his closing-the-deal smile.

"I don't seem to have much of a choice, do I?" Rage and sorrow combined forces to make India shake. At least she could feel the shaking. She had no idea if it was visible.

Somehow she found the willpower to take a couple of steps back out of their way. She tried not to hate them as they passed her, checking out the floor, the intricate moldings at the edge of the walls, the pressed-tin ceilings. After all, she couldn't blame them for inquiring about buildings on the market.

No, this was all Celene. And the more she heard, the more India stewed. The more she stewed, the more she wanted to go give Celene a piece of her mind. Maybe it was a good thing that the duo of Sladen and Raybourn were here now because otherwise she might march down the street and give Celene Bramwell a giant chunk of her mind. And that would just prove that Celene had been right all along, that no matter how much you dressed up India Pike she was still poor white trash at her core.

Justine paused for a moment as she followed the men. "I'm so sorry."

All India could do was nod.

Once Justine and the men were in the other room, Skyler touched India's arm.

"You need to sit down."

"What I need is to tell Celene what a bitch she is."

"As attractive as that might seem, not the best idea. We'll figure out a way to fix this."

India met Skyler's eyes. "How? She knows I don't have the kind of money it would take to buy one of the spaces, let alone both of them."

"A loan from the bank, maybe?"

"The way lending is now?" India shook her head, hating how defeated she felt.

"Don't give up yet. I promise, we'll figure this out."

India's outlook changed from one moment to the next, making her feel a bit schizophrenic. First she wanted to agree with Skyler, buckle down and find a solution like she always had when faced with a challenge. But then a sliver of the insecure girl she'd been would surge to the surface and punch her self-confidence in the nose.

She glanced toward where Justine was showing the men around. India couldn't hear what they were saying, and honestly she didn't want to. Instead, she needed to focus on her next step. Because no matter what doubts were making a reappearance, she was not going to go down without a fight. She'd worked too hard to build her business, the life she wanted. There was no sense in trying to figure out why she suddenly felt as if she were being bombarded from all sides, because the why didn't matter. What did matter was what she was going to do about it.

Another incredibly long minute ticked by before Skyler stepped in front of India, blocking her view of the men. "I have to get back to the inn for a meeting now, but I'll call you later, okay?"

"Yeah. Thanks."

Skyler hugged her before heading back to her own job. For a few seconds, India envied her friend. Skyler owned the Wildflower Inn. Unless she didn't pay her taxes or went bankrupt, she didn't have to worry about someone waltzing in and taking it away from her. Skyler was much too meticulous to let either of those things happen.

India wandered behind the front counter, not wanting to even see the men who had the power to destroy everything. Her jaw tightened as she stared out the window at her neighbors walking up and down the sidewalks. Scenarios for making the best of a bad situation began to run through her head. Maybe she would go to the bank and apply for a loan. Sure, she doubted it would be approved, but she wouldn't know for certain until she tried.

And if that didn't pan out, maybe the suited duo would decide not to buy and that would give her more time to move on to whatever option number two ended up being.

But what if they did buy the buildings and evict her? Could she find another space? It certainly wouldn't be as prominently placed as where Yesterwear sat now, right in the heart of the downtown that drew tourists.

She tried not to think that this might be the world's way of showing her that Blue Falls wasn't where her future lay. She didn't even want to entertain that thought. It was too easy to run away.

Justine, Kevin and Mark walked back into the small front room. Mark thanked her again before he held open the door for Justine. But Kevin motioned for them to go on and he'd catch up.

"We seem to have gotten off on the wrong foot," he said as he leaned one hip against the counter.

"It's safe to say I didn't expect someone to possibly be buying my business out from under me."

"How about you let me take you out to dinner to apologize for upsetting you?"

She eyed him and realized he was everything she'd always said she wanted in a man. Good-looking, well dressed, successful. But an image of Liam popped into her mind, nudging Kevin aside even though he was still in front of her.

She should say yes to Kevin's invitation. Maybe an evening with someone like him would shove all her annoying daydreams about Liam out of her brain. And if he ended up owning her building, maybe she could convince him to at least let her keep the space she had. Despite all that, she found herself shaking her head.

"Already taken," he said. "I should have known."

Instead of correcting him, she couldn't make herself say anything.

"Well, if that ever changes, you let me know." With a wink and a smile, he headed out the door.

As if she were sending out bad vibes, the store stayed empty most of the afternoon. The more she sat and thought about what Celene had done, the more she fumed. But instead of giving in to the urge to go scream at Celene about the unfairness of the situation, she channeled her energy toward an action plan. First up, her case for the bank to grant her a loan.

But when she went to the website for Justine's real estate listings, her stomach did a nosedive. The price tag for even her building was hefty. Could she risk losing everything by going into debt up to her neck with a big mortgage payment in addition to the one on her cute little house?

She looked around her at all the items she'd carefully selected to showcase in Yesterwear, thought about the thrill she experienced when she discovered a new designer and inspired designs. She couldn't give this up, not without a fight.

An hour before her normal closing, she packed up her purse and the bank loan form she'd downloaded and filled out, doing her best to cast herself and the business in a positive light. Instead of driving, she headed down the sidewalk toward the bank. It wasn't that far, and she needed the time to try to rein in her nerves. She hadn't been this nervous since she'd signed on the dotted line to lease the space for the store.

Well, that wasn't exactly true, was it? Every time she was around Liam Parrish, her nerves sparked like an entire package of firecrackers set ablaze.

But this was different. This was her livelihood, her

future, her life's work. Liam was simply a man passing through a tiny sliver of that life.

For some reason, she felt a pang in her chest at that thought. It was enough to make her falter. She took a deep breath. She didn't need to be thinking about Liam, his tall, lean body, those beautiful eyes of his.

Oh, for heaven's sake, she had somehow lost a grip on her nice, orderly life. It was as if Fate decided she needed to shake things up a bit just for fun.

As she walked into the bank, she stood straight and made sure her steps were confident. She crossed the lobby of the Blue Falls Bank, straight to Kim Stegall's office. She tapped on the edge of the open door.

When Kim looked up, she smiled, lighting up her fair face and green eyes. "Hey, India. I was just thinking about you."

Was that good or bad? "Oh, yeah?"

"I saw that darling set of boots you have in the window, and I can't stop thinking about them. I've walked by them every day this week, telling myself I don't need them, that I don't need one more pair of shoes."

India smiled as she pictured the two-tone, brown leather-and-suede ankle boots. "There is no such thing as too many shoes."

"I'm not sure my husband would agree. He thinks the shoes in my closet are having illicit affairs at night and producing more shoes."

India laughed but had to force herself to focus on the business at hand when the words *illicit affairs* bounced around in her head, accompanied by the image of Liam that just refused to keep its distance.

"Is there something I can do for you?" Kim asked.

"Yes, actually." India moved into the office and took

a seat on one of the chairs facing Kim. "I'd like to apply for a loan."

"How much are we talking?"

"Enough to buy the building my store is in." She wanted to ask for enough to buy both spaces, but that really was beyond the realm of possibility. Before Kim could shut her down on the spot, she handed over the printout from Justine's website with the listing for the building along with a detailed accounting of India's qualities that made her and her store a good investment.

Kim took a couple of minutes to look over everything while an entire flock of butterflies fluttered away in India's stomach. She went back over every detail in her mind, the financial reports for the business, how she'd never missed a rent payment there or a mortgage payment on her home, her good credit score, her plans for making the business even more successful. With the extra space slipping away, she'd spent some time planning how she might rework her current space to make it even more attractive to customers.

When Kim finished going over all the information and didn't immediately meet India's eyes, the butterflies kicked it up a notch.

"This all looks very good, India."

India's heart dropped into her stomach. "I'm sensing a 'but' coming."

The apologetic look on Kim's face when she finally looked up wasn't that different from the one Justine had worn when she'd brought Kevin and Mark into the store. "I hate doing this, but I know a loan of this size won't be approved."

"What did I do wrong?" It wasn't what she'd meant to say, and India hated how desperate she sounded. But she'd come to the end of her rope.

If possible, Kim looked even more sorry. "Nothing.

That's the thing. A few years ago, this most likely would have been approved. But times have changed. It's much harder to get approved, even for small loans. And this is no small loan."

"So there's no chance?"

Kim looked as if she was breaking the news to a little kid that Christmas had been canceled. "No, I'm sorry. I really am. I know you have a great business. Maybe the building won't sell, or the new owners will allow you to stay. After all, you're a good tenant."

A tenant, what she'd been her entire life. Even now, with a business of her own, someone else had the power to uproot her.

India's eyes began to burn. She had to get out of the bank before she started crying. She stood. "Thank you for seeing me."

When Kim extended the papers to her, India shook her head. "Just shred them."

By the time she hurried out of the front door of the bank, she had to blink against the tears. Once outside, she looked up at the sky, the wide, blue expanse mocking her. Anger churned inside her, and before she could tell herself what a terrible idea it was, she headed down the sidewalk toward Celene's store, her chunky heels clonking against the concrete.

She rounded the corner at Peach and Main and promptly slammed right into someone, hard. In the space of a breath, she gasped and tried to take a step back, only to twist her ankle and fall in an inglorious heap on the sidewalk.

"God, India, I'm sorry."

Through her blurry, teary vision, she realized the person now crouching in front of her, the person she'd slammed into like a runaway train, was none other than Liam Parrish. Just what she needed.

"Are you hurt?" he asked.

Was she? It took a moment for the pain in her ankle and rear end to register, quickly followed by a flood of embarrassment. Could this day get any worse? She cursed under her breath and swiped at the tears.

"I'm fine." But when she tried to stand, she rethought that assertion. Pain shot up the leg from her twisted ankle.

"Here, let me help you," he said as he put his shoulder under her arm.

She wanted to decline his help, but she wanted to stop making a spectacle of herself even more. He lifted her with such gentleness that more tears formed in her eyes. Once she was on her feet, he still didn't let go.

"Can you stand by yourself?"

She did her best to stand on her own two feet, but the moment she put pressure on the injured ankle she winced.

Liam tightened his grip on her. "Come on, let's get you back to your shop."

"No. My car. I just want to go home." And curl up with the tub of orange sherbet in her freezer.

"I have a better idea," he said. Liam started walking down the sidewalk, supporting almost all of her weight.

Even though she winced every time she stepped with her injured foot, India also grew more and more aware of the feel of Liam's arm wrapped around her back. He wasn't a beefy guy, but it was obvious he was strong. She guessed he'd have to be to hang on while a bronc bucked him this way and that.

Liam steered her to the left, and that's when she saw his truck parked on the side of the street in front of the hardware store. She couldn't help but think how it probably bugged Celene to no end that the downtown sported a hardware store in among the "more appropriate" establishments.

"I can drive myself home," she said.

"I'm sure you can," Liam said, but that didn't divert him from what he intended. He opened the passenger-side door and edged her toward it.

India balked and met his eyes. He was close, so close she feared his nearness might intoxicate her.

He leaned a little closer, not taking his eyes from hers. "Want me to pick you up?"

She narrowed her eyes but gave in, using the handle above the door to pull herself inside the truck. Liam shot her a victorious smile before he shut her door and rounded the front of the truck.

She dared not look at the shop windows lining the street. No doubt at least a few eyes had seen her fall, noticed when the handsome cowboy lifted her to her feet then deposited her in his truck. Were her neighbors wondering why she'd allowed him, where they were going, if there was something going on between them?

So what if there was? It wasn't as if sticking to her life plan had turned out so well.

She shook her head, trying to clear out all of the negative thoughts. If she gave in to them, they'd infect everything in her head. She'd lived in that space once upon a time, and she never intended to go back. For those angry moments between leaving Kim's office and when she'd crashed into Liam, her anger had eclipsed her common sense.

Liam slid into his seat and started the truck's engine so the air conditioner could begin cooling off the interior of the truck's cab. "Where were you going in such a hurry?"

"To do something very stupid. I suppose I have you to thank for getting in my way."

He tipped his hat. "Here to serve, ma'am."

His exaggerated drawl made her laugh, something that hadn't seemed possible only minutes before.

"That's more like it," he said. "So, where to?"

She gave him directions to her house on Verbena Lane. "Where's Ginny?"

"At a reading program at the library with Mia." He glanced at her. "Thank you for introducing them. They're inseparable now."

Her life might be falling apart and her ankle throbbed as if it had its own heartbeat, but the thought of Ginny and Mia becoming besties made her smile. "I'm glad."

When Liam pulled up in front of her house, however, another pang of worry overtook her as she looked at the little white house with the gardens of wildflowers she'd planted. She had to find a way to ensure the safety of her business. Otherwise, she'd be in danger of losing her home, as well.

"Why am I not surprised you have a white picket fence?" Liam said as he put the truck in Park and cut the engine.

India shifted her gaze to him. "What does that mean?"

He held up is hand. "Nothing. It looks nice, perfect."

Did she imagine a bit of extra inflection on that *perfect?*

Liam got out of the truck and headed to her side. She didn't wait for him, instead opening the door and slipping out onto her uninjured leg.

"There's nothing wrong with wanting things to look nice," she said.

"No." He didn't elaborate, and for some reason that annoyed her more than if he had.

But what did he know about pretty things? He spent his days around dusty barns and smelly animals. There was absolutely nothing wrong with trying to make your surroundings as beautiful as possible. It made her happy, and it didn't hurt anyone. And she didn't have to explain it to Liam Parrish.

IT DIDN'T TAKE A GENIUS TO figure out that India was not having a good day. The first clue was the anger that had been fueling her when she'd barreled into him, then the tears that for some reason he thought had more to do with her anger than the physical pain of her injury. Now she was just irritated, probably because her ankle prevented her from stalking off and leaving him behind.

He pushed the passenger-side door of the truck closed and once again put his arm around her so she didn't have to put her full weight on her injured ankle. "Come on, Hopalong."

"Oh, very funny," she said, but behind the annoyance was a hint that she wanted to laugh.

"I seem to keep rescuing you from your feet."

She swatted him on the arm, but there wasn't much force behind it. "You seem to be the reason I always end up in a foot-related crisis."

He knew it wasn't what she meant, but he kind of liked the idea of her feet getting tangled and her not remembering how to walk when she saw him. The mere idea made him smile.

"What are you smiling about?" she asked as he helped her up onto her front porch, complete with a white porch swing.

"Nothing."

"I don't believe you."

He looked at her. "Then you'll just have to wonder."

She gave him a mutinous look that made him laugh then dug in her purse for her house key. She didn't hand it to him, instead opening the door herself and hobbling inside. She didn't invite him in, but he followed, anyway.

"Um, make yourself at home," she said sarcastically.

"Don't fuss. I'm just making sure you're settled and have everything you need before I go. Never leave a damsel in distress."

"I can manage."

He crossed his arms as she continued to stand instead of sitting like a normal person. "Anyone ever tell you that you're stubborn?"

"I prefer self-sufficient."

"No, stubborn."

She made a sound of frustration. "What, you're going to wait on me hand and foot?"

He shrugged. "Maybe a little."

She glanced toward the door. "What about Ginny?"

"She won't be finished for another half hour."

India tossed her purse on the glass-topped coffee table and shoved her hands onto her hips. "I don't think I'm the only stubborn person here."

"Nope, you're not. Only difference is I admit it." With that, he nodded toward the couch. "Sit. I'll fix you an ice pack."

"Liam—"

"Sit before I pick you up and put you there myself."

India threw her hands up but finally stepped to the couch and sank down. "Satisfied?"

"Yes." With a smile he suspected would irritate her further, he headed into her kitchen. When he spotted a bread bag with only a few slices of bread in it, he dumped out the bread and filled the bag with ice from her freezer. He grabbed the towel hanging from the stove handle and wrapped the ice pack inside it.

"What are you doing?"

Oh, this had to upset her perfect little world, having someone stroll into her home and take over. Well, she could handle it for a few minutes.

He walked back into the living room, straight to the couch. He took one of the decorative pillows and laid it flat. "Put your foot up on this."

To his surprise, she did exactly that without an argument. He positioned the ice pack on her ankle so that it wouldn't slide off.

"Is that the bread bag?"

"Yep."

"But it had bread in it."

"Bread that will be sandwiches shortly."

With a sigh, India lay back on the couch, her head resting on yet another of the silky white pillows. He never would understand why people had little cutesy pillows everywhere, especially ones with tassels and beads like these.

When he returned to the kitchen, he gave it a closer look. Like everything else he'd seen about India Pike, it was in perfect order, as though it could be on the front of one those home magazines at the grocery checkout. Pale yellow walls with white cabinets and trim, polished silver handles on the cabinets and drawers, new appliances, and not a dirty dish in sight. He shook his head and couldn't imagine his home ever being this spotless. Single dads didn't have homes for the cover of magazines unless it was *Disorder Digest*.

Inside the fridge, he found a container of lunch meat and condiments. He put together a couple of turkey sandwiches, but placed a plate with lettuce and tomato slices and some condiments on a tray he found on top of the fridge. He added a couple of bottles of water and retraced his steps back to the living room.

India was still lying on the couch staring at the ceiling. He couldn't say what it was, but there was something vulnerable about the look on her face, as if she were all alone. He resisted the crazy urge to pull her into his arms, to make her feel safe.

"How's the foot?" he asked instead.

"Throbbing less." She hesitated for a moment. "Thank you." She sounded as if it was hard to say, as if she wasn't used to needing help or accepting it.

He pushed aside some sort of decoration on the coffee table. Honestly, it looked like a dugout canoe filled with carved wooden balls. He set the tray down on the now empty space.

India pulled herself up to a sitting position, leaving her foot elevated on the pillow. "Why are you doing this?"

Liam sat in the red-and-white-checked chair adjacent to the red couch. "What should I have done, India? Left you sprawled on the sidewalk?"

"No, but—"

"But what?"

She opened her mouth but hesitated, as if searching for an answer. "I just don't like depending on anyone else."

"Everybody needs help sometimes."

"I doubt you ever ask for help."

"That just shows you know nothing about me." He leaned forward and slapped some mayo, lettuce and tomato on his sandwich, then took a big bite.

India made her sandwich without a word, but once she had it in her hands she didn't bring it to her mouth. Instead, she stared at the tray. "I'm sorry."

"For what?"

She glanced up at him. "For being so bitchy. I've just had the worst day."

"I suspected by the way you were steaming down that sidewalk earlier." He rested his forearm on the chair's arm, his half-eaten sandwich in his hand. "So what 'stupid' thing was it that I kept you from doing?"

Instead of answering, India took a bite of the sandwich, chewed it slowly then swallowed. With a sigh, she sat back from the edge of the couch. "I was about to let go of my temper and cuss someone out."

"Now there's something I can't imagine, you cussing."

"I don't make a habit of it, but if I get angry enough, I've been known to let a few words fly."

"Wasn't me you were going to cuss out, was it?"

She looked startled by his question. "No, why would you think that?"

He shrugged. "Just get the feeling sometimes that I'm not your favorite person."

"I...I've just been under a lot of stress lately."

"And I added to it?"

She shook her head. "No, it's just I already had work and the next BlueBelles class, and then the rodeo got dumped on top of that. Not that I mind, I want to help Mia any way I can."

"Let me guess, you're one of those people who can't say no to volunteering."

"I just like to do my part."

"Uh-huh."

She didn't bother arguing with him, probably because he was right.

They ate for a bit in silence, and his eyes roamed the room, at everything in its perfect place. A well-kept houseplant with not a dead leaf in sight. A painting of bluebonnets hung expertly on the far wall. A few picture frames along the mantel, but not so many that it looked cluttered. Two magazines on the opposite end of the coffee table that didn't look as if they'd even been opened, let alone dog-eared.

"So what's a BlueBelles class?"

"An enrichment class for young girls. Skyler, Elissa and I host them, and we cover different topics each time we have them. We're trying something new this next time, the day before the rodeo. We're going to have a day full of different presentations and classes." She turned toward him suddenly. "Ginny should come. I bet she and Mia would enjoy it."

"Is this more of the dress-up stuff?"

"Sometimes we do something related to fashion, but that's not all it is. This time we have a native plant gardening class. Elissa owns a plant nursery, so she's doing that. One on self-esteem. A lady who owns an art gallery in town is doing a painting class. It'll be fun."

"I'll think about it. We might be in West Texas. I may have to cancel that cake for Ginny's birthday. Her grandparents are lobbying hard for me to bring her over for a visit for her birthday."

"The day before the rodeo?"

"Yeah."

"That's a lot of driving in a day's time."

"Yeah, but we haven't been out there since last summer. They came to Fort Worth at Christmas."

India picked at the edge of her sandwich. "Would they come here?"

"I don't think I can fit my entire family in the RV."

"No, but Skyler owns an inn. I'm sure she'd give a good rate since you're working so hard on the rodeo. And you could even have the party there."

His instinct was to refuse, but he realized that would be no different than India not wanting to accept help. He could afford to put his family up at a nice place and rent a room for the party. "It sounds nice. I'll check it out."

India lowered her injured foot gingerly to the floor and faced him. "I could put it together if you want."

He smiled. "There you are, volunteering again."

"True, but it's the least I can do for the guy who has saved me from my own klutziness, twice."

"It was my pleasure." He said the words before he thought about them, but he realized they were true. Something about India made him want to be there to catch her every time she fell, no matter how independent and capable she was. To try to push those types of thoughts out of his head, he went for teasing. "Maybe it's time to think about safer shoes."

"You may be right."

But contrary to his words, he really liked seeing her in those impractical heels. They did nice things for her legs, legs that he had the sudden urge to feel wrapped around him. Unnerved by that burst of desire, he stood suddenly and grabbed the tray. He carried it back to the kitchen and returned the supplies to the refrigerator. After he was done, he took a moment to lean his hands against her sink and look out the little window above it. Even her backyard looked immaculate, with perfectly trimmed grass, a white gazebo and big pots of purple flowers spilling over the sides.

He couldn't imagine living like this, afraid to leave an inadvertent smudge or a wrinkle. He thought of Charlotte, of her designer clothes and expensive scent. She'd been flawless in appearance. It was what was inside that needed some work. He wouldn't try to fit into someone else's world, one where he didn't belong, again.

Still, India wasn't Charlotte, was she? Could he chance letting himself think that way? Because this couldn't possibly work out in the end, no matter how much the image of her had filled his head since his arrival in Blue Falls. No matter how much he wanted to stalk back into the next room, lay her flat on that couch and kiss her until all her stubborn resolve fell away.

Chapter Nine

India stared toward the doorway that led into her kitchen, wondering why it was taking Liam so long to come back. He wasn't making any noise, so what in the world was he doing? Just as she was about to ask him, she heard his footsteps. She shifted her gaze away from the doorway and straightened the items on the coffee table.

Liam walked into the room, and she couldn't keep herself from looking up and staring at those long legs encased in denim. Luckily, his back was turned to her as he examined the items on her mantel. She was torn between wishing he would hurry up and leave, and acknowledging that a sliver of her wanted to find out what would happen if he spent the night.

"You were a beauty pageant queen." It wasn't a question. He said it as if it weren't a surprise at all, but she wasn't sure he considered it a good thing.

"The Belle of Blue Falls," she said. "Elissa and Skyler wore that crown the two years before."

He turned halfway toward her, the picture in his hands. "Three peas in a pod."

"They're very good friends." If not for them, her teen years would have been so much worse.

He stared at her for a moment, as if he could see deeper into her than what her words should have revealed. It scared her that she had the sudden urge to tell him everything. Instead, she forced her mouth to stay closed.

She was saved by the fact that he turned his back to replace the framed photo of her in her crowning moment.

"I better go get Ginny. Will you be okay?"

"Yes."

He turned and headed for the door. He had the door open before she found her voice again.

"Thanks. Contrary to how I acted earlier, I appreciate the help."

For a split second, he looked surprised. But then he nodded. "You're welcome."

It wasn't until he'd driven away that she realized she had no way to get to work the next day.

THANKS TO THE ICE PACK and staying off her foot all night, India's ankle felt much better the next morning. It wasn't even swollen or bruised. She had Liam to thank for that. If he'd let her stubbornness rule the day, she likely would have had a lot more pain this morning. Still, she wasn't going to risk heels today. Instead, she pulled out a pair of copper ballet flats that matched a sleeveless, satin top. She normally wore it with a cream skirt, but when she spotted a pair of jeans hanging at the back of her closet she found herself pulling them from the hanger.

For today, just today, she was going to dress down a bit. At least dressing down for her.

She still hadn't decided whom to call for a ride to work. No matter what number she dialed, the person on the other end of the line was going to have questions. She had no doubt that word of her fall and subsequent departure with Liam was already making the rounds. Honestly, she was surprised Elissa or Skyler hadn't called her yet.

Her decision ended up being made for her. The sound

of a car door outside drew her to the window of her bedroom. She spotted Verona headed up the walkway to the front door. India reached the door and opened it before Verona had a chance to knock.

"Should you be on that foot, honey?"

India stuck out her leg and wiggled her foot. "Good as new."

"Well, someone must have a healing touch."

India knew exactly whom Verona meant and that she was fishing for information. "Nothing a little ice and rest couldn't cure." She grabbed her purse and scooted out the door, locking it behind her.

The fact that Verona didn't keep asking questions as they slipped into the car and headed downtown made India nervous. Questions, she was prepared for. This silence, not so much. It wasn't until Verona turned onto Main that she spoke again.

"So, it seems Liam was at the right place at the right time."

"Not sure he'd feel that way. I did, after all, slam right into him."

"Yeah, he said you were in a big hurry."

India glanced at Verona's profile as she stopped at a red light. "You talked to him?"

"Yes, saw him at the library picking up his little girl yesterday. Said he'd just come from here, and that you'd need a ride to work since you would probably be stubborn enough to not skip a day of work."

Now wasn't the time to be skipping work. If anything, she needed to work harder to boost her business. If Kevin and Mark, or anyone else, bought the building, she needed to do everything in her power to make them want to keep Yesterwear as a tenant. Plus, there was the not-so-little part of her that didn't want Celene to think that her decision to sell had made India so distraught that she couldn't even manage to come to work.

When Verona pulled into a parking space in front of the shop, India reached for the door handle.

"Thanks for the ride."

Verona took India's hand, stopping her. "Why don't you try to get to know Liam more? Maybe if you give him a chance, you two might find out there are some sparks between you."

India placed her other hand atop Verona's. "I appreciate your concern, but I'm not in the market for a man, not right now, anyway."

Verona held her gaze for a long moment. "Be careful you don't wait too long, or you might wake up someday and realize you're old and alone."

India would swear she saw genuine sadness in the other woman's eyes. But then Verona retrieved her hand and shifted her gaze forward, India's cue to get out of the car. Even after she was out on the sidewalk and watching Verona pull away, she couldn't shake the feeling that Verona hadn't just been issuing a generic warning. It was as if she was speaking from experience. Verona had always seemed like one of the happiest people in the world, but she'd never married, never had children of her own. Was she always trying to help others because she was lonely?

India headed inside, but as she worked throughout the morning she kept thinking about Verona and what she'd said. Was she right? Would India end up alone because she never took a chance?

But even if she did decide she could take that chance, shouldn't it be with someone like Kevin and not Liam? Or had she just told herself that for so long that she'd convinced herself it was the truth?

The door opening drew her attention. A teenage girl

walked in, and it took India a moment to place her. "Hello, Lara. How are you?"

"Good, thank you."

"Can I help you with something?"

"I'll just look around a bit, if that's okay?"

"Sure. Take as long as you like." India deliberately made herself seem busy, allowing Lara to wander through the racks of clothes to her heart's content. She knew Lara couldn't afford anything in the store, hadn't been able to even before her parents' house had been struck by lightning and burned to the ground.

India's heart squeezed, feeling a sudden kinship with this young girl who was by all accounts a sweet person and a good student. No, their parents were nothing alike, Lara's being hardworking ranchers. India's parents had been takers, moochers on society. Lara's were proud, unwilling to take help even when most people would. India had heard Lara was staying in town with her grandmother while her parents gradually rebuilt.

When Lara finally wandered back to the front of the store, she hesitated at the end of the jewelry counter. "Can I have a job application?"

India's first instinct was to think that she couldn't afford to hire anyone, but she stopped herself when Verona's words echoed in her head. Even if Liam wasn't part of her future, maybe a little more freedom was. Maybe if she had a little help, she wouldn't be so stressed. And she thought of how she'd longed to be able to get a job when she was Lara's age. Even if she hadn't lived so far out of town to make it impossible, she doubted anyone would have hired her.

"I actually don't have any, but that doesn't mean we can't talk about anything that would be on it." She motioned toward the table at the back of the entry room. "So you're looking for a summer job?"

"Yes, ma'am."

India made a dismissive wave. "None of that 'ma'am' stuff. I'm not that much older than you."

Lara smiled, and it showed just how pretty she was. Her long blond hair was pulled back in a braid, and she had the body of a runner. If India remembered correctly, Lara was on the local high school's cross-country team.

"Have you applied any other places?"

Lara's smile faltered some, as if she thought India was trying to gently guide her in a different direction. "No. I came here first. It's the coolest store in town."

India knew within a couple of minutes that she was going to hire Lara. Even if the building was bought and they kicked Yesterwear out, surely they'd at least give her three months to find an alternate location and make the move. That would give Lara the summer of employment she needed, and India would feel good about doing the right thing even if it did put a ding in her bank account.

"When can you start?"

Lara's eyes widened. "Does that mean I got the job?"

"Yes, it does."

Lara looked as if she wanted to jump up and hug India, but she managed to stay seated. India's heart swelled with happiness. This turn of events was unexpected, but it felt like just the thing that needed to happen to her today. She felt lighter and freer already, which was odd because she'd never felt trapped by her job and responsibilities.

"As soon as you'd like me to," Lara finally said.

"How about right now? I'm going to order some lunch from the Primrose," India said as she stood. "What would you like?"

"I don't need anything."

India walked toward the phone behind the front counter. "Nonsense. It's my treat, your welcome to the job. Plus, I need someone to split a piece of pie with me. If I keep eating full ones, I'm going to be as big as the town water tower."

She placed the order, gave Lara a few quick instructions in case anyone came in while she was gone, then headed to the Primrose to pick up the food.

The moment she stepped in the front door of the café, her gaze settled on Liam. And on Gretchen Toliver's hand resting on his shoulder. A wave of jealousy slammed into her with such force that she found herself striding across the dining room and plopping herself down in the empty chair between Liam and Ginny.

"Hey, India," Ginny said, her face brightening.

India patted Ginny's hand. "Hey, sweetie. How are you?"

"Good."

Out of the corner of her eye, India saw Gretchen retrieve her hand.

"I think your order is ready," Gretchen said.

India met the younger woman's eyes as if nothing out of the ordinary was going on. "Great." But she didn't move to the counter where she normally picked up her to-go orders.

After a moment's hesitation, Gretchen headed toward the pickup window.

"Your ankle must be better," Liam said.

"It is, thank you." She let her gaze stay locked with his for a moment longer than usual. She thought she saw a question before Ginny spoke again, drawing her attention.

"Dad says I'm going to have my birthday party at your friend's hotel."

"Is that right?" India glanced at Liam.

"I talked to Skyler this morning, got everything worked out."

"Will you come to my party, India?"

India smoothed some fuzzy hair atop Ginny's head. "If you want me to."

Ginny nodded.

"Then I'll be there."

Gretchen approached the table with two large and one small to-go boxes. "Here's your order."

India wondered if Gretchen knew how obvious she was being about her attraction to Liam. A shot of fear went through India. Was she acting the same way? In an effort to make sure she wasn't, she handed over her money to Gretchen. "Keep the change." She stood, not so quickly that she looked nervous but not so slowly that she seemed reluctant to leave. "Well, work calls."

And then she ran away while trying not to look like that was exactly what she was doing.

LIAM WATCHED INDIA LEAVE, feeling a little as though he'd been picked up by a tornado and almost immediately spit back out.

"Do you like India, Dad?"

He jerked his gaze away from India, realizing he'd been staring too long. "She's nice."

"No, silly." Ginny shook her head as if he were as dumb as a box of rocks. "Do you like her like boys like girls?"

"How do you know about boys liking girls?"

Ginny rolled her eyes. "Katie has a boyfriend," she said, naming her best friend back home.

"A boyfriend, in second grade?"

"I'm in third grade now."

"Oh, excuse me, third grade." Why did kids always want to grow up so fast? Not that he had been any different.

"Well?"

"Why do you want to know?"

Ginny shrugged and looked down at her empty plate.

"Honey, is something bothering you?"

"I don't know." Now she sounded very much her age

instead of a teenager masquerading in a nearly eight-year-old's body.

"Did someone say something to you?" If Verona or one of India's matchmaking friends enlisted his daughter in their plans, he wasn't good with that.

"No."

He wanted to keep pushing, but he could see Ginny closing in on herself. She rarely talked about not having a mother in her life, but was she getting to the age when she'd miss having a mom even more? He thought back to the day when she and Mia had such a good time playing dress-up at India's. Ginny had always been his little tomboy, but what if she only did that to make him happy? That would break his heart. But the thought of her becoming more like a little girl scared him, too. He didn't know how to be a parent to a regular girl. What if he did it all wrong?

"How about we go down to the bakery and pick out what kind of cake you want for your birthday party?" Even though India had said she'd get to it, she had too much on her plate to worry about picking a cake for a kid she barely knew.

"Okay," Ginny said.

As he'd hoped, her mood brightened again. She hopped up from her chair, ready to go. He laughed and tossed the money for their bill and a generous tip on the table and let Ginny pull him out the front door and down the street toward the Mehlerhaus Bakery.

As they neared the bakery, he spotted India standing in front of her store talking to a man in a suit. He couldn't hear a word they were saying, but he knew instantly he wouldn't like it if he did. Because judging by body language alone, the guy was flirting with her. It proved way more difficult than it should be for him to stick to his side of the street. India's flirtations and dating life were none of his business.

Then why was it also difficult to concentrate as Ginny and Keri talked about possible cake designs? Why did he keep glancing out the window and fighting the urge to tell the guy to back up, to put more distance between him and India?

"What do you think, Dad?" Ginny asked, dragging his attention back where it should have been in the first place.

"What, sweetie?"

Keri pointed toward a cake design in the book on the front counter, a princess in a blue dress.

"Sure, whatever you want. It's your birthday."

As Ginny wandered over to the display case to look at cupcakes, Keri closed the book of cake designs but didn't take her eyes off Liam.

Liam pulled out his wallet and handed her a credit card.

As Keri ran it through the card reader, she glanced out the front window. "They're not a couple," she said. "Not that I don't think he's trying."

"Excuse me?"

"India and the guy she's talking to, just in case you were wondering."

"I wasn't."

"I don't believe you."

Coming from most people, her words would have annoyed him. But there was something about Keri that he liked. She came across as a no-nonsense kind of woman, one who said what she thought without trying to beat around the bush. He respected that.

"And India's a good catch," Keri said.

"I don't think we have much in common."

"You can't know that until you really get to know a person, can you?"

He opened his mouth to say something, but his brain

fritzed out on him. The only thing that bubbled up was that he did want to ask India out, against all logic.

Keri handed his credit card back to him. "Take it from someone who knows. Sometimes we're destined to be with the one person we're sure isn't for us."

Keri's words banged around in his head all afternoon as he got back to work supervising the replacement of some of the lights and checked out the sound system at the rodeo arena. Maybe if he just stayed away from India, he could get through the rodeo and return home to where he'd evidently left his sanity. But damned if he didn't look up to see her driving into the fairgrounds.

Was the damn universe trying to tell him something?

She waved when she got out of her car and started walking toward him.

He glanced at her flat shoes. They weren't exactly sturdy, but at least they weren't heels. Maybe she'd stay on her feet today.

She eyed the arena behind him. "Everything's looking great."

"Yeah, we're almost ready, which is good since competitors will start rolling into town in a few days."

"I came by to see if you needed anything else from me because I'm going to be busy with some other things for a while."

His jaw stiffened when he thought that maybe the guy in the suit was one of those things. But maybe all she meant were the events occurring alongside the rodeo, maybe her class for little girls. "No. You've done your part on the rodeo."

She nodded and looked past him toward the barn. "That's a pretty horse."

"Yeah, that's Mars." He glanced toward where he'd left his horse tied to the hitching rail outside the entrance to the barn. "I had a friend trailer him down this morning since he was already on his way to Bandera to pick up another horse."

"He's huge."

"But a total softie. Come on and say hello." Liam headed toward the big roan but looked back when he noticed India hadn't moved.

"He looks like he could squish me."

"But he won't." Liam extended his hand, and after a moment's hesitation and to his surprise, India took it. He was struck again by the dainty softness of her skin, but he liked it.

When they got close to Mars, Liam felt a shiver go through India. "I promise he won't hurt you." He took India's hand and placed it against the side of the horse's neck.

"It feels softer than I imagined. I thought horsehair was coarse."

"It can be, but I take very good care of my animals. And Ginny loves brushing the horses. They probably love her more because she babies them."

India looked up at him and smiled. "And you let her."

"Yeah." He watched as India tentatively moved her hand along Mars's neck. "So tell me how a Texas girl manages to never ride a horse, especially when you live in an area surrounded by ranches."

India's hand stilled, but she didn't remove it from the horse. "We didn't have horses, and I never really had the opportunity to be around them much. The one time I was at someone's house who had a horse, it tried to bite me."

"You'll be happy to know Mars isn't a biter, not even if you feed him. Want to try?"

India retrieved her hand and took a step back. "I don't think so."

"As I tell Ginny, you won't get over a fear unless you

face it." Not giving her a chance to think about it, he retrieved a bucket of grain hanging just inside the barn and extended it to her. "Go ahead, fill up your hand and hold it out to him."

"Really, I don't think this is for me."

"I promise he won't bite. And if he does, I'll let him bite me, too."

The expression on her face told him she was conflicted. At least some part of her wanted to face her fear. Finally, she took a tentative step forward and dipped her hand into the bucket. With her palm full of grain, she edged it closer to Mars's mouth. When she got close, she closed her eyes as if she didn't want to see the monster horse teeth preparing to chomp off her fingers.

Liam placed his hand against her back to comfort her. At least that's what he told himself. The fact was he liked touching her, and the more he did the more he wanted to. And he had no idea what he was going to do about that.

Chapter Ten

India tensed when she felt the warm breath of the horse against her hand, scared half to death that she was about to lose her fingers. She yelped when Mars touched her, but Liam's hand at her back steadied her. At least as far as her fear of the horse was concerned. If she wasn't so concerned about the horse, she was sure she'd freak out more about Liam touching her.

"It's okay," Liam said. "Open your eyes."

She barely opened one and peeked out. What she saw made her open both eyes fully. Mars was eating out of her hand, barely nuzzling against her palm with his soft nose. She laughed at the sight, at how she was doing something she would have bet everything she owned she would never do.

"He's so gentle," she said.

Liam scratched the big horse between his ears. "He's a good boy, aren't you, buddy?"

India watched, fascinated. She even got up the courage to stroke Mars between his big, brown eyes.

"See, not so bad, huh?" Liam smiled at her, as though he were proud of what she'd accomplished.

"No. But don't expect me to be barrel racing anytime soon."

Liam laughed, and she couldn't help thinking that she'd miss the sound of that laugh when he left Blue Falls.

"How about a little ride to start off?"

"What?"

"A ride, up the trail." He pointed toward the trailhead at the edge of the fairgrounds, the one that wound up into the hills. "I took him for a short ride when he got here, but he needs to work out more of the kinks from the trip here."

"You want me to get on top of a horse?"

"I bet you'll love it. Nothing like it in the world."

She glanced back at the RV. "What about Ginny?"

"She's at Mia's house. Jake says having her around keeps Mia's mind off the upcoming treatment."

"That's good, for both of them."

Liam placed his hand on the saddle. "So, no, you can't use my kid as an excuse."

"I don't know. Letting Mars eat out of my hand is one thing. Trusting him not to kill me is quite another."

"Mars has never thrown me, never put me in any danger."

"Yeah, but he's used to you. Can't horses sense fear?"

"He won't act any differently than normal because I'll be with you."

"Oh." The thought of Liam riding so close made her skin warm. She hoped he would attribute any evidence of that to the heat of the day.

Before she could say anything else, Liam positioned her at the side of the horse. "Put your hands on the pommel," he said, patting the saddle part in question.

She opened her mouth to decline, but Verona's words echoed in her head again. So she let him help her scramble onto the saddle. She was sure she looked like a fish trying to ride a bicycle. "Wow, that was graceful."

Liam laughed as he effortlessly pulled himself up behind

her. "You didn't end up off the other side on your face, so I call it a win."

India figured she would have laughed if she'd had any breath left. The feel of Liam's long legs alongside hers, the way he was pressed close behind her, completely wiped out her ability to think coherently, to speak nothing of normal breathing and heart rhythm.

When he wrapped his arms around her to take the reins, she sucked in a breath before she thought how that might sound.

"You okay?" Liam asked.

"Yeah, just nervous." And not just about being way up on a horse, either.

"Nothing to be nervous about."

Did he have to say that so close to her ear? The man must have been clueless if he couldn't figure out how that might affect her. Of course, she hadn't given him any reason to think she might be interested, had she? In fact, quite the opposite.

She still didn't know if she could risk letting her guard down, but she found she wanted to more and more each time she saw Liam. Not even Kevin's second attempt to get her to go out with him that afternoon could keep her mind from wandering to Liam in the middle of that conversation. As if she were somehow attuned to his presence, she'd noticed him across the street as he and Ginny had stepped into the bakery. She'd been surprised by how much she wanted to get rid of Kevin so Liam wouldn't get the wrong idea.

With a gentle nudge, Liam set the horse in motion. India clung to the pommel so tightly it bit into her palms.

"You're not going to fall. I won't let you. Trust me."

He couldn't know how much those last two words scared her. Trusting people wasn't something she'd ever been particularly good at, not when the two people she should have been able to trust the most had failed her so utterly.

"So how long have you been riding?" she asked, trying to focus her attention on something other than her fear or the feel of Liam's thighs pressed against hers.

"Since my first memories," he said. "I grew up on a ranch way out in West Texas, and my dad had me on a horse before I could walk. Heck, before I could crawl."

"But you decided not to be a rancher."

"No. I guess it was one of those classic 'can't wait to get away from the middle of nowhere' stories. I hit the rodeo circuit pretty early. The road appealed to me, even though riding resulted in a few broken bones, a couple of concussions, more bruises than I can count. If not for Ginny, I might still be on the road full-time. Even with her, I can't totally give it up. I get to missing it."

"So you compromised with running your company?"

"You could say that, but I like it, too. Keeps me in the business, even when I'm not riding."

"I guess you had Ginny riding pretty young, too."

"Yep. I have this picture of us on a horse when she was a month old, our first picture together."

"What, no pictures of you holding the pink, wrinkly newborn?"

She couldn't tell for sure with the movement of the horse, but she thought she felt Liam stiffen for a moment.

"I wasn't there when she was born."

"Oh, sorry. Didn't mean to pry."

"No apology necessary." He guided Mars off the trail onto a flat, open area. "See anything familiar?"

"You can see right down Main Street from here. I had no idea."

"I'm guessing you've never been up here. Not exactly a trail for high heels."

She swatted his arm, eliciting a laugh.

"So what do you think of your first horseback ride so far?"

"It's nice." She leaned forward and rubbed the side of Mars's neck. "You were right about him."

"I'm right about a lot of things."

India turned halfway and gave him a raised-eyebrow look. "That so?"

The moment his gaze met hers, she wondered if she'd made a mistake making eye contact.

"It is." His words didn't sound like playful banter anymore. "Like I think the two of us should go out tonight."

"What?" Didn't she sound like a genius, as if she couldn't grasp the meaning of his words?

"Out to dinner."

She broke eye contact and turned back around to stare down at her hometown, the town Liam was just passing through. "Is this part of your plan to get Verona and the others to lay off the matchmaking?"

"No. I just want to take a beautiful woman to dinner. Simple as that."

"Oh."

Liam laughed. "You sound surprised."

"I am."

"Are you really?"

"Yes. I didn't think you liked me very much."

"Do you think I take women I don't like on horseback rides?"

She shrugged. "I suppose not."

"So that's a yes?"

"I didn't say that." She squirmed on the saddle but froze when her bottom bumped back into him. She gulped at the hardness she felt there.

"Then it's a no."

She licked her lips and swallowed against the dryness invading her throat. "I didn't say that, either."

"Then what are you saying?"

She shook her head, unable to think clearly. "This isn't a good idea."

Liam placed one of his hands on hers and squeezed gently. "India, it's just dinner. We've both been working hard, you probably more than me since you have so many irons in the fire. I think we've earned a night off and a nice meal, don't you?"

She took a deep breath. "Well, if you put it that way, I guess I could eat."

"Good answer. Guess we should get back then unless you want your date smelling like a barn."

India had the strangest, most-unlike-her feeling that she'd like Liam Parrish just fine, no matter how he smelled.

IF INDIA DIDN'T STOP PACING her living room, she was going to dig a trench right down the middle of the floor. She looked at her cell phone again, considering whether she should call Liam and cancel. Yes, it was cutting it close. He should be here any minute. But could she really go out with him and maintain her resolve to keep things on a professional level? Because she didn't want to allow herself to fall for him, not when everything about giving in to her temptation felt as if it would end in disaster. And, honestly, she had enough potential disaster hanging out on the horizon.

No, she couldn't go through with this. Better to just keep things how they were, get through the rodeo, and he'd be gone. Then maybe she could refocus all of her energy on figuring out the best way to ensure the security of her business.

She'd dialed the first two digits of Liam's number when she heard his truck pull into her driveway. She stood frozen, halfway to the third number, as she listened to the sound of his truck door closing.

She canceled the call and closed her eyes. When had she become such a chicken? She was perfectly capable of having a meal with a man without it having to mean more than friendship. She was strong enough to manage it tonight even though she was insanely attracted to Liam. It wouldn't be the first time she'd hidden her true feelings.

After he knocked, she waited a couple of seconds before moving toward the door. She didn't want to seem too anxious to see him. The friendly, casual greeting that was on her lips died when she saw that he'd replaced his usual jeans and button-up shirt with a dark suit, crisp white shirt and deep blue tie.

"I never thought I'd say this, but you're a bit underdressed for dinner," he said with a mischievous smile.

She looked down at her white slacks, gold sandals and tan top with a Cleopatra-style neckline. Then she looked back at Liam, just in case she'd imagined the suit and tie. Nope, still there.

"I think maybe you're a mite overdressed for the Primrose."

"We're not going to the Primrose."

"Um, the other choices are even more casual than the Primrose."

"Not in Austin, they're not." He glanced at his watch. "If we're going to make our reservation, you'll need to hurry. I couldn't get anything later."

"Where are we going?"

He leaned toward her a little. "It's a surprise," he said in a faux whisper.

Stunned, she turned halfway and motioned for him to come in. "I'll be as quick as I can."

Once inside her bedroom, she closed the door and leaned

against it. Never in her wildest dreams had she imagined Liam showing up dressed more like Kevin and whisking her off to a fancy restaurant. It was a step closer to what she'd said she always wanted, and it freaked her out.

After taking a few deep breaths, she crossed the room to her closet and shuffled through her array of choices. When she spotted a simple black dress with a black satin ribbon circling the waist, she pulled it from the closet. You couldn't go wrong with a little black dress.

She hurriedly changed and slipped on a pair of black satin Mary Janes and some onyx-and-diamond earrings she'd bought for herself to celebrate the opening of her store. It'd been a luxury she could ill afford at the time, but it had seemed important to mark the occasion with something a little more substantial than a celebratory piece of pie.

As she placed her hand around the knob on her bedroom door, she stopped and considered the choice for her earrings. She didn't wear them often, so why now? She had others that would go with the dress. It felt almost as if she were placing too much importance on this night, this date with Liam. She considered changing the earrings, then scolded herself for overthinking yet again.

Liam was right. She had been working hard, and she deserved a night to enjoy herself. If it happened to be with the sexiest man she'd seen in, well, maybe forever, that was just the cherry on top. She opened the door and walked into the living room where Liam stood looking at the other pictures on her mantel.

When he turned to look at her, something flickered in his eyes. She wasn't so out of touch with the dating world that she couldn't recognize male interest in a woman when she saw it. Her nerves threatened to derail her, but she gave them a mental slap and told them to leave her alone.

"You look beautiful," Liam said.

"Thank you. And I should have said it before, but you look very handsome. I wouldn't have guessed you had a suit stashed away in that RV."

"I didn't."

He'd bought an entirely new outfit just to take her to dinner? Her heart fluttered in her chest, tempting her to believe that maybe this might be the beginning of more than just a friendly dinner.

Liam extended his bent arm. "Shall we?"

India stepped forward and took his arm until they reached the front door. He opened it for her then stood at the bottom of her front step as she locked up. He offered his hand to help her down a step she'd negotiated countless times.

He smiled. "You never know when a high heel might rebel against you."

"And here you were being such a gentleman until now."

He laughed as he placed her hand in the crook of his arm and escorted her to his newly washed truck. It wasn't an expensive foreign car or a limo, but she couldn't have felt any more special if it had been.

She marveled at this new side of Liam Parrish as he drove them east toward Austin. He was still as ruggedly handsome as ever, but there was no hint of the rodeo cowboy tonight. She was surprised to find that she missed that side of him a little while still being able to appreciate how nicely he cleaned up.

As he guided the truck along the highway, she showed him some points of interest and he told her about some of his rodeo adventures.

"Have you ever thought about quitting?"

"There were a couple of times. Once when I got bucked off this horse named, appropriately, Mean As a Snake.

Broke my arm in two places, and part of the bone came out the side of my arm."

"Ugh, that sounds horrible."

"Wasn't my favorite day."

"So what was the other?"

He didn't immediately answer. She was beginning to think he wasn't going to as they entered the edge of Austin, and he took a series of streets to get to the downtown area.

"It was when I got Ginny."

"Got her?"

She noticed a subtle tightening of his jaw.

Liam took a deep breath and let it out slowly. "I didn't even know Charlotte was pregnant. Then one day she showed up at the rodeo in Cheyenne with this little bundle and thrust it at me along with legal paperwork naming me as the father and relinquishing all rights to Ginny."

India stared at Liam's profile, stunned by his words. "She didn't want her?"

"No. She'd slept with me on a dare from some of her sorority friends. They'd driven up to Cheyenne from Denver as a joke, to see how many of them could 'bang a rodeo cowboy' in one night. I should have known better. She'd looked as out of place as a peacock on a chicken farm, not the kind of woman you'd expect to even see at a rodeo, let alone slumming with a cowboy."

"Don't say that."

He glanced over at her. "That was her point of view. I knew that the moment she handed over Ginny as if she was no more than an annoyance she was glad to be rid of."

"That's awful. I can't imagine doing that."

"Most decent people couldn't." He pulled the truck into a parking space in a small lot next to a brick building.

India looked up and saw the sign. "We're going to Clementine's?"

"Yeah. I hope that's okay."

"More than okay. They have some of the best food in the city."

"That's what I heard."

As Liam got out of the truck and came around to her side, India felt as if her emotions had just taken a spin on a Tilt-a-Whirl. She went from nervous about the upcoming evening, to surprised by the effort Liam had evidently gone to in order to make the date a nice one, to aghast by the story Liam had told her about Ginny's mother. How could a woman be so cold as to just hand off her newborn to a man she didn't really know as if the baby were no more than a sandwich she didn't want? India really hoped that Ginny didn't know the full truth about her mother.

Despite all her work with the BlueBelles classes, India had never really and truly pictured herself as a motherly type. But in this moment, she wanted very much to pull Ginny Parrish close and make her feel as if she were the most special little girl in the world.

After they made their way inside and were seated at their table, India looked at the menu but had trouble focusing on the options. She kept thinking about what Liam had told her.

"I shouldn't have told you about Charlotte."

When she looked up from her menu, she noticed Liam watching her. "No, it's okay. I…I just can't wrap my head around it. Did she say why?"

"It 'wasn't in her life plan.'"

"Well, that's a pitiful reason." But was she much different? She'd resisted even admitting an attraction to Liam just because he didn't fit perfectly into her life plan. She shook her head and consulted the menu again. Her dedication to hard work and long-held goals was not the same thing as handing off a baby like a baton in a relay race.

After they ordered, India found herself at a loss for something to say. A flicker of panic lit inside her. How were they going to fill the coming hours before they returned to Blue Falls and she could retreat to the safety of her home?

"Can I ask you something?" Liam asked.

"Sure."

"Why the store full of fluffy stuff?"

"Fluffy stuff?"

"You know, female froufrou."

She smiled at his description, at the way he seemed to be at a loss for how to accurately describe Yesterwear. "What should I be selling instead, horse tack?"

"I'm thinking that wouldn't be a good fit."

She picked at the edge of the cloth napkin in her lap. "I've always liked watching old movies, seeing what the actresses wore. I guess I'm just fascinated with the styles of the past and how they can be applied to modern fashions." When she saw the confused look on his face, she laughed. "Did you understand a word of what I just said?"

"About half of it."

She needn't have worried about how they'd fill the time while they ate. Stories about Ginny's antics mixed with her own about how the BlueBelles classes came about entertained them both. What took the cake, however, was Liam's tale about the time he made it to the National Finals Rodeo in Vegas and how a female Elvis impersonator had proposed to him.

"Let's just say she'd had more than a few drinks and she smelled like it, too."

India laughed so hard that she snorted, then covered her face in embarrassment. Of all the places to snort, she'd let loose in the restaurant where the governor of the great state of Texas was dining three tables away.

Liam's grin stretched from ear to ear, and she was glad

to see it. Since he'd told her about Charlotte, she could tell those memories had been there on the periphery, though he'd done his best to hide that fact.

After they finished dessert and Liam paid the bill, he guided her toward the door with the gentle placement of his hand at the small of her back.

"Thanks for dinner, Liam. It was wonderful."

He gestured toward the park across the street. "Feel up to a short walk? The air's more pleasant tonight than it's been in a while."

"Okay."

A thrill went through her as he took her hand in his and led her across the street. He didn't let go once they were in the park, on the path that led to the river. They passed other couples holding hands, and a flush of happiness filled India that she was in the company of such a handsome, nice man.

"Do you mind if I ask you something else?" he asked as they reached the river. He guided her to a little gazebo that sat just above the rolling water.

"Go ahead."

"The day you ran into me, you said you were going to cuss someone out. Who was it?"

India retrieved her hand from his and walked to the edge of the gazebo. She placed her hands on the railing and looked out toward the rising moon and its reflection on the water. "My landlord."

"Upping the rent?"

"No, she's selling the building, and she didn't tell me it was even on the market. I found out about it when the real estate agent brought potential buyers into my store to look around."

Liam moved next to her and leaned back against the railing. "Little lacking in the communication department."

India shook her head. "It's more than that. I've been

after Celene for months, nearly a year to lease out the space next door so I can expand. But she basically patted me on the head and told me to be grateful I even have what I do."

"If she wanted to sell, why didn't she offer it to you?"

"I'd like to say it was because she knew I wouldn't qualify for that size of loan, but it's more than that." India stared at the moon on the water again, watching the ripples make it dance. "Celene Bramwell is a Class A snob. She comes from money, and she's known me long enough to know that I don't."

"Most people don't."

"A fact that no doubt bugs Celene to no end."

"No offense to Blue Falls, but it seems like an odd place for someone that uppity to live."

"She came with her husband from Boston years ago. He passed away, but she never left. I've come to believe it's because she likes to be a big fish in a little pond, a pond that she has every intention of remaking into her own little version of Boston."

"I would think she'd like a store like yours."

"Oh, she's one of my best customers. I'm fine to help her when she's trying on clothes and tossing aside half my stock when she's done. I just shouldn't dream so big as to want more."

Liam edged closer to her and placed his hand on hers. "India, what is it?"

She looked down at his hand and resisted the urge to turn hers over and entwine her fingers with his. "It's nothing. Sorry to be such a downer all of a sudden."

Liam lifted his other hand and cupped the side of her face. "It's not nothing."

She looked at him then, met his eyes in the faint light shed by the moon and the lampposts in the park. "You thought I was like Charlotte, but I'm not. She had money, didn't she? Lots of it, I'm guessing. Well, I didn't. I grew up with nothing. Everything I have, I've worked long and hard for. You asked me earlier why the froufrou. Because from my earliest memories, I've wanted to bring beauty into the world."

Liam's hand slid up her jaw, and he caressed her cheek with his thumb. "There's already beauty in the world. You just have to know where to look."

He lowered his lips toward hers, and India was so stunned that she couldn't move. When his mouth captured hers in a soft, tender kiss, she didn't immediately kiss him back. But one more careful movement of his lips against hers, and she was a goner. She lifted her hand to the back of his head and pulled him closer. Then she kissed him with all the desire she'd been trying to deny ever since he'd strolled through the front door of her store and turned her life upside down.

Chapter Eleven

Liam pulled India closer and ran his fingers through her long hair. She tasted of cinnamon apples from the tart she'd had for dessert. Her body fit so nicely against his, causing his heart rate to increase and other parts of him to sit up and take notice, too.

He felt the moment she began to pull away even before she broke the kiss. She looked dazed and at a loss for what to do next. He knew exactly what he'd like to do next, but that wasn't a good idea. Already, he'd done more than he'd intended. But he wasn't sorry, not one bit.

"Are you okay?"

She nodded. "Yeah. I think I'm just way more tired than I thought. Been a long day."

He knew it was more than that by the way she refused to make eye contact. She was pulling inward, and he didn't know if it was something he'd done, if he'd pushed her too far. If she hadn't kissed him back the way she had, he might have believed she wasn't interested in him. But you didn't kiss someone like that if you didn't want to. Unless, of course, he was a terrible kisser. Not that he'd ever had any complaints, not even from Charlotte.

No, something else was going on and he was smart enough not to push for the answer, at least not now. Instead, he took her hand and led her from the gazebo back onto the path through the park.

The drive back to Blue Falls was quiet, at times too quiet. But each time he tried to start a conversation, India would give only the bare minimum response and then go quiet again. He glanced over to see her leaning her head against the passenger window, so maybe she was simply tired as she claimed.

He was almost glad when he finally pulled into her driveway. He wasn't what you'd call a chatterbox, but he'd never been a fan of tense silence, either. After putting the truck in Park and cutting the engine, he reached for his door handle.

"I had a nice time tonight," India said, drawing his attention. Her hand was on her door handle, as well. She wasn't going to let him walk her to the front door.

Had he misjudged her interest earlier? Had she only been curious about kissing him and now she'd satisfied that curiosity? He didn't like how that made him feel, and his hand tightened on his door handle.

"I did, too." What else was he supposed to say? How would she take it?

Before he could answer his own questions, she opened her door.

"Good night."

Resigned, he released his door. "Good night, India."

He started the truck and turned the lights back on, but he didn't pull out of the driveway. Part of him wanted to jump out and race to her front porch before she could get inside, pull her close and kiss her again, long and deep and thorough. But that obviously wasn't what she wanted. Still, he couldn't leave until he saw that she was safely inside. At the last moment before she slipped out of sight, she turned and waved. And then she was gone.

For a few seconds, he couldn't move. But finally, he put the truck in Reverse and backed out of the driveway. Glad that Ginny was spending the night with Mia, he drove slowly toward the fairgrounds with the window rolled down, hoping the wind would knock some sense into him. What was he doing getting involved with someone he'd probably never see again after the rodeo was over? Hell, that was more a move out of Charlotte's playbook.

No matter how much of a fool he told himself he was, he still couldn't manage to stop thinking about India as he parked next to the RV then walked to the barn to check on the horses. When he finally stepped into the RV, it seemed incredibly empty. He sat on the edge of the bed and damned if he didn't imagine India in it with him, her beautiful dark hair tousled and fanning out over his pillow as he made love to her.

"Damn it," he muttered and rubbed his hand over his face.

He undressed, tossing the new suit he'd bought to impress her on the couch. He flopped back on the bed and stared at the ceiling, wondering what in the world he should do next. Did he even know what he wanted? He cursed himself for letting India get under his skin. Pretty sure he wasn't going to come up with any answers tonight, he closed his eyes and tried to will himself to sleep. Maybe some magic would happen overnight and he'd have the answers he needed in the morning.

INDIA FELT AS IF SHE HADN'T slept in a month. She supposed that was what she got when she let down her guard and kissed Liam as if they had some kind of future together. They didn't, and she had to nip whatever this was between them in the bud before her feelings deepened any further. She'd had quite enough heartbreak in her life, and she'd become an expert on making sure it didn't happen again. And that meant no more kissing Liam, no matter how much she'd liked it.

She hadn't been at the shop five minutes when Skyler and Elissa showed up. Even though they had a scheduled meeting for last-minute details on the BlueBelles classes, one look at their faces told her that wasn't the main topic on their minds.

"Yes, I went out with Liam last night," she said before they could ask. "I'm not even going to ask how you found out."

"How was it?" Elissa asked, obviously excited about the news.

"Nice. And it was a one-time thing."

"Must not have been that nice."

Skyler swatted Elissa's arm then turned her attention to India. "Why not?"

"Because I've got way too many other things to worry about right now. I don't need to be wasting time going out on dates when I have a business to save, classes to plan, a rodeo to make sure is successful."

"Well, the classes will be over soon, and the rodeo right after that," Elissa said as she propped her elbow on the top of the jewelry case.

"And then Liam goes home to Fort Worth," India said.

"So that means you can't have fun while he's still here?"

India lifted her gaze to Elissa's. "Yes, it does. You know I'm not into casual dating."

"No, you want to save yourself for Mr. Right. You know what I think? That you've built up this idea of the perfect man in your mind to a point where you'll never find anyone to fit the bill, especially not in Blue Falls. And that's been the point all along. If you never get involved with anyone, you can never get hurt."

"Elissa," Skyler said in a tone that urged her to stop talking.

"No, it needs to be said. You know I love you like a sister, India, but I've watched you live in a shell for a long time without saying anything. It's not healthy."

"And dating every man who crosses your path is?"

Skyler extended a hand to both of them. "Stop, both of you, before you say something you'll regret."

Elissa tossed her notebook on top of the jewelry case. "My parts of the classes are ready to go, but my notes are in here if you need to check anything." She pushed away from the counter and headed for the door.

"You're leaving?" Skyler asked.

"Yeah, I don't think I'm India's favorite person right now."

Before India could consider how she felt about Elissa at the moment, her friend stepped out the door and strode away down the street.

Skyler turned slowly back toward India, that uncomfortable look of being caught in the middle on her face. "Are you okay?"

India didn't answer immediately. Instead, she let her gaze roam over the entry room to the store, at the clothing carefully displayed, toward the double glass doors that led into the room where they held the BlueBelles classes. "What if she's right?"

"Do you think she is?"

India returned her gaze to her friend and shook her head. "I don't know."

"Then I think that's something you should figure out."

If it were only that easy.

LIAM PARKED ACROSS THE STREET from Yesterwear and wished he didn't have to get any closer. But he'd told Ginny she could attend the BlueBelles classes when he'd run into Elissa the day before and she'd asked Ginny if she was going. Even though he suspected Elissa was still in matchmaker mode, still following in her aunt's footsteps, he couldn't very well tell Ginny no, could he? Not when there wasn't a good reason for her not to attend other than his conflicted feelings about India.

Sure, he hadn't called her since their date, but he'd not gotten the sense that she wanted him to. Why couldn't women just come right out and say what they wanted? Then maybe he could figure out what the hell he wanted.

Ginny opening her door prompted him to get out of the truck. With her hand in his, they crossed the street. Once they were standing outside the store, he let go of her hand.

"Have a good time today. I'll pick you up when you're done."

"Okay. Bye, Daddy." Ginny started toward the front door.

"Wait, no kiss goodbye?"

"Oh, yeah." Ginny spun and hurried back to him.

He tried to quell the flash of resentment that his daughter was so excited to get inside that she'd nearly forgotten their typical goodbye ritual. Already she'd dressed differently today than she normally did with him. Instead of her usual jeans, boots and shirt, she wore one of the outfits his mother had bought her for school. The one nicer outfit he always insisted she bring on their trips in case they had to dress up for some reason, the one she never wore when they were on a rodeo location. But he hid his feelings and smiled at her before planting a kiss on her forehead. Then he presented his cheek, and she gave him a quick peck before hurrying inside. He couldn't help the feeling, however irrational, that he was losing his little girl.

"What, not going inside?"

He turned to see Verona stepping up next to him.

"I think I might stick out like a sore thumb in there."

"I don't know. A handsome cowboy such as yourself might be a little more than welcome."

He glanced in the front window and caught a glimpse of India.

"Well, don't keep an old lady waiting in suspense. You never know when my time might run out. How did the date go?"

Liam wasn't even surprised Verona knew about the date. Heck, it was probably front-page news in the local paper. "It was nice, but I don't think India is interested in a repeat."

"But you are." She didn't ask, instead stating it as fact.

He shifted his gaze to her, and she gave him an understanding half smile.

"Don't look so surprised. You're wearing your interest right out here where anyone can see it."

"I know you mean well, but I think this is one match that isn't going to be made."

"Oh, no. I'm not giving up yet, and neither should you."

When he started to speak, she held up a hand to stop him. "I know very well what India probably did. She started to open up a bit and then got scared and closed down faster than you can say 'snap.'" Verona snapped her fingers to accompany her words. "I'm the first to say that she's got plenty of reasons for having those walls, but those reasons aren't mine to share. I do know it's high time she realized she's found someone it's worth letting those walls down for."

Liam shook his head. "How can you say that? You don't really even know me. I could be the most horrible guy in the world for her."

"The simple fact that you said that proves to me you're not. Plus, all I had to see was you with your little girl. A man who is that good of a father is one worth his weight in gold. Or barbecue, depending on the mood you're in."

Liam couldn't help but laugh. "You're quite a woman, Verona."

"So is India. That's why I'm telling you not to give up. Keep hammering away at those walls of hers until you break through."

He looked through the window again and saw Skyler and India ushering the little girls into the back room. "If I really care, I'd just leave things as they are. I'm leaving in a few days."

"That's why my tax dollars build roads. If two people like each other, things have a way of working out."

Liam wasn't sure it was quite so simple, but he couldn't deny that he wanted to find out.

INDIA TRIED NOT TO BE obvious as she watched Liam walk across the street, back toward his truck. A painfully lonely part of her wanted to race out the door and into his arms, to feel his lips capture hers again. But instead she stayed rooted where she was, growing more miserable by the moment.

Skyler wrapped her arm around India's shoulders and gave her a quick squeeze. "You know I am not the best at relinquishing control, but what if it's worth taking a risk?"

"It just doesn't make any sense. Maybe if he lived here, maybe if we weren't so different. But I just don't think physical attraction is enough."

"From the outside looking in, I don't think that's all that's going on here." With another squeeze, Skyler let go and took a step away. "But I won't push. Only you will be able to figure out when it's the right time to take that chance, if you ever want to." With that, Skyler returned to the classroom.

Across the street, Liam pulled away from the curb.

The door opened again, and Elissa stepped halfway inside before glancing over her shoulder just as Liam drove by.

Caught in the act of watching him, India turned her back, afraid of what had shown on her face.

Elissa approached and stopped beside her. "I don't like us being upset with each other."

India took a couple of moments to answer. "Me neither."

"I'm sorry. I still think what I said was true, but I could have found a better way to say it."

"No," India said, surprising herself. "You were right. I do try to protect myself, but I don't know if I can stop."

"You just take a leap of faith. And even if the worst happens, your friends are here to pick you up." Elissa reached over and took India's hand. "You're not alone anymore. You haven't been for a long time."

She heard the words, knew they were true, but India still didn't truly believe she could let go of the way she'd learned to protect herself so long ago. But she guessed all she could do was try the same way she'd built a life for herself once she was on her own and in control of it—one step at a time.

THE NEXT DAY, INDIA SWITCHED from BlueBelles mode to that of rodeo wrangler. Well, helping Skyler, Elissa and Verona wrangle fair vendors, anyway. One moment it was telling the funnel-cake maker where to park his truck, and the next it was helping Keri hang a sign for the cupcake contest on the front of her bakery tent or showing the members of the high school football team where to set up their lemonade stand.

By the time they got the final vendor settled, India was dog-tired. She sank onto a lawn chair alongside her friends.

"We really are suckers for volunteering, aren't we?" Elissa said.

All India could do was make an affirmative sound as she watched another truck pulling a horse trailer enter the fairgrounds. The field on the opposite side of the fairgrounds was now covered with trucks, trailers and RVs.

"It looks like half of Texas is here," Verona said. "I may pass out from watching all these good-looking men."

"Woman, most of these guys are young enough to be your kid, maybe even your grandkid," Elissa said with a playful nudge to her aunt's arm.

"Honey, I'm old, not dead."

India found the energy to laugh. The laugh died in her throat when she saw Liam walk out of the barn. She'd seen him several times throughout the day, but nothing more than a single wave had passed between them. She guessed that was her answer as to whether she should take that leap of faith.

"Liam sure is a sexy thing," Elissa said. "So, India, you never did tell us. Is he a good kisser?"

India leveled her gaze on her friend.

"What, you thought I was going to give up?" Elissa smiled. "You know me better than that. It's in the gene pool."

"One of these days, all this meddling is going to backfire on you," India said.

"You didn't answer the question."

India rolled her eyes. "If I answer, will you lay off?"

"Nope."

India threw her hands up in defeat. "Fine. He's a great kisser. Satisfied?"

"Why, yes, I am."

After a few more minutes of rest and listening to her friends rate the cowboys they saw on a scale from one to ten, India stood. "I've got to go take a shower and get ready for the party. I really hope that's in your futures, too," she said as she scanned her equally hot and sweaty friends.

She had to keep reminding herself that she would get through the next few days one step at a time. And tonight's step was Ginny's birthday party at the inn. Then the rodeo and related festivities, after which Liam would roll out of town and she could go back to her normal life, one that was still up in the air.

When she arrived at the inn a couple of hours later, the first person she saw was Kevin.

"For me? You shouldn't have," he teased.

She lifted an eyebrow. "You get a lot of packages with big pink bows, do you?"

"I'm not picky if there's something good inside."

"Afraid it's not your size."

"I guess I'll forgive you if you will finally agree to go out with me."

"You are nothing if not persistent."

"You're a successful businesswoman. I suspect you must have a streak of persistence, too."

India decided to take the opportunity he presented to shift the topic of conversation. "Speaking of my business, have you decided to buy my building yet?"

"*Your* building?"

"I've come to think of it that way even though my name isn't on the deed."

The door to the lobby opened behind them, prompting Kevin to place his hand on her shoulder to ease her out of the way. She glanced to her left to see that it was Liam who'd walked in. The question in Liam's eyes made it difficult to smile at him, especially when Kevin was still touching her. She took a subtle step to the left to break the contact, but Liam had already looked away and headed across the lobby as if it hadn't mattered to him at all.

As she watched him stride away, she wondered how quickly she could drop off Ginny's gift and beat a retreat.

"I think I see the reason you've been declining my offers to take you out," Kevin said.

She shifted her gaze back to him. "No, I'm just busy."

He didn't look as if he believed her, not about Liam, anyway, but she acted as if she didn't notice.

"So, the building?"

Kevin shoved his hands into the pockets of his dark pants. "We haven't decided. Still running numbers and checking out other properties."

"Here in Blue Falls?"

"Other places in the Hill Country." He grinned. "But if I thought there might be another reason to choose Blue Falls over the other towns, I might lean this direction."

"I'm sorry, Kevin. Now just isn't the right time. My main concern is if I'm going to have a place to conduct my business by this time next month."

Kevin's expression dimmed some, the teasing gone. "That I can't tell you."

India's heart sank, but at least she could respect his honesty. "Well, if you'll excuse me, I have a birthday party to get to."

"Have fun." With that he headed for the front door.

India took a deep breath, prepping herself to be in the same room with Liam, and walked toward the path he'd taken moments before.

When she entered the banquet room, it had been turned into party central. Skyler had outdone herself with pink-and-white balloons, a big bowl of frothy pink punch, bite-size sandwiches, mini tarts, the cake Keri had made front and center and a large sign that said, "Happy Birthday,

Ginny!" hanging from the far wall. You'd think she'd known Ginny all her life. But that was Skyler, always going the extra mile to make sure her guests felt special.

Those guests included a man who made all of the circuits in India's brain go wonky, a man who currently was talking to an older couple. His parents, she guessed. She watched the older man and realized that he looked like an older version of Liam with white hair and a deep tan that spoke of the time he spent outdoors under the Texas sun. He was still handsome, as Liam would be. India couldn't stand to watch them anymore because she knew that Liam would just be a distant memory by the time she reached the age of the elder Parrishes.

She turned her head and spotted a table covered in presents. As she made her way toward it, Elissa and Skyler came through the doorway that led to the inn's kitchen.

"Hey, about time you got here," Elissa said. "Thought you were going to be a no-show."

"I've been here a few minutes. Just ran into my potential new landlord in the lobby, and figured it wasn't a good idea to ignore him."

"Have to say he's been getting a lot of appreciative stares from the women staying here," Skyler said.

"I wish he'd return them."

Both of her friends looked at her with curious expressions.

"He's asked me out three times already. He doesn't seem to want to take no for an answer."

"Well, aren't you popular all of a sudden?" Elissa teased with a wink.

"Yeah, where was that in high school?"

"Seriously, you were better off not going out with those guys," Skyler said.

"Hey, not all of them were bad," Elissa said.

"You're just saying that because you went out with them," Skyler countered.

"Is it Pick on Elissa Day or something?"

"If it's not, it should be," India said.

"Two against one, no fair."

"Them's the breaks, babe," Skyler said, then barely moved out of the way of Elissa's friendly whack with a party noisemaker.

Skyler nodded toward the other people in the room. "Come on. Time to party."

Ginny looked away from her grandfather and spotted India. Her face brightened so much that India's heart hurt. It was amazing how much she liked this little girl. When Ginny waved, Liam and his parents looked toward India. Feeling as if she didn't have an option, she crossed the room to them.

"Hey, India," Ginny said.

"Hello, and happy birthday."

Ginny smiled. "Thank you." She looked up at her grandparents. "This is the lady with the cool store where Mia and I played dress-up."

"Oh, we've heard all about you," Liam's mother said as she extended her hand. "I'm Annabelle Parrish."

India took the older woman's hand and shook it. "It's nice to meet you."

"And this is my husband, Jack."

India shook Mr. Parrish's hand, too. Up close, he looked even more like Liam. She dared a look at Liam to find him watching her.

"Looks like Skyler pulled out all the stops for the party," she said.

Liam glanced around the room. "Yeah. You all didn't have to go to this much trouble."

"It's no trouble." India caressed Ginny on the top of her

head then wondered if she should have. Would the Parrishes think more was happening here than there was?

"We hear you're the one planning this rodeo," Jack said.

"Not really. I'm just handling a few details. Liam is the one really putting it together."

"Don't let her fool you," Liam said. "She's worked like crazy on this."

India's heart lifted at his praise. She looked at him and smiled. The tension that had formed between them since their date eased a little.

"How about we open some presents?" Elissa said as she stepped up between Jack and Liam, causing Liam to take a step toward India. Elissa made eye contact with India and gave her a quick wink.

"Yay!" Ginny said and hurried with Mia toward the table with the presents.

Liam and Jack followed the girls, leaving India standing beside Annabelle.

Suddenly nervous, India forced herself not to fidget. "Have you had a chance to get out and see Blue Falls yet?"

"No, we'll poke around a bit in the morning before we head home. I want to check out this store of yours. And I hear there's a marvelous bakery."

"Yes. Keri made the birthday cake."

"We met earlier. Lovely girl, with such a cute little one."

Ginny dug into her presents with enthusiasm and impatience. She got coloring books and crayons from Mia and her dad, a little camera from her grandparents, a purple backpack full of books from Skyler and Elissa, and a stuffed bear from Verona.

"Well, you've got plenty to keep you busy on the road," Jack said.

India winced at the thought that soon Liam and Ginny would be gone. How could she get so attached to them in so short a time? Unable to help herself, she looked at Liam. He was watching his daughter with a smile of pure happiness on this face, his parents flanking him. She sensed so much love among the four of them that it brought tears to her eyes. She blinked them away before she had to explain why she was crying at a child's birthday party.

There were only two packages left, and India expected Ginny to pick the one from her next. Instead, she chose the one that had to be from Liam. She ripped the paper covered in brightly colored birthday cakes off the box to reveal a red cowgirl hat. India's breath caught when she realized it perfectly matched the boots she'd bought for Ginny.

Ginny plopped the hat on her head and smiled from ear to ear. She hopped up and gave Liam a big hug.

Drat, there were those tears again. Across from where she stood, Elissa noticed and gave her a "What's wrong?" look. India shook her head and shifted her attention back to Ginny, who was grabbing the final present.

When she finally got the box open, Ginny made a sound of appreciation. Then she grabbed the boots and held them up. "Look, Daddy. They match my hat!"

"I see that." Liam made eye contact with India, but only for a moment.

She couldn't tell what he thought of the present, but there was no mistaking Ginny's appreciation as she ran to India and hugged her.

"Thank you. I love them."

India bit her lip before patting Ginny on the back. "You're welcome, sweetie."

"Well, I don't know about anyone else, but I think it's time for some cake." Skyler walked by and touched Ginny on the shoulder, guiding her toward the cake table.

When Skyler met India's eyes, India saw that her friend knew how close she was to tears. Ginny's affection had almost sent her over the edge. How was this child burrowing herself so deeply into India's heart?

Skyler cut pieces of cake and handed them out. India stared so intently at her own slice that she didn't notice Liam approaching until he was right next to her.

"That was a very nice gift you got for Ginny."

She found the strength to look up at him. When their eyes met, she couldn't help remembering their kiss and wishing it would happen again. "I'm sorry if you think it was too much. I sometimes go a little overboard."

"You didn't have to spend so much, but she obviously loves the boots." Liam watched his daughter laugh as she shoved chocolate cake in her mouth.

"Not the type of thing I usually buy, but I thought they were something she'd actually use."

Liam gave her a bit of a funny look she couldn't decipher before he looked away as someone turned up the music that had been playing in the background.

Jack swept Annabelle into his arms and spun her around in time to the music. The way he looked at his wife, as if he were just as in love with her as the day they married, felt like a punch in the chest to India. It wasn't that she wasn't happy that this couple still held so much love for each other. It was just that it reminded her of how she used to wish her parents were more like the Parrishes.

She swallowed hard as Liam took a couple of steps and swept Ginny up into his arms and danced with her, making her giggle. Jake Monroe danced with Skyler, and with a dramatic bow Elissa swept Verona into the whirl of dancers.

India hated to leave without saying goodbye, but she felt her resolve to stay cheerful breaking. If she didn't get out of this room soon, she would make a complete fool out of herself.

But that was what she was, a fool for falling for a man

with whom she had no future. Caring for a girl who wasn't her daughter and never would be. Wishing a couple she'd just met could be her parents. She set her half-eaten cake on one of the tables and headed for the door while everyone's attention was directed elsewhere.

Chapter Twelve

Liam finally relented to Ginny's laughing pleas to set her down. But he stole a kiss before he let her go to play with Mia. He looked back toward where he'd left India to find her hurrying out the door. He took a step to follow her before he pulled himself up short.

"Is something wrong with India?" his mother asked from beside him.

"Probably just tired. Long day today, and more on tap tomorrow." He knew in his gut that something else was going on, but it wasn't his place to ask what. His jaw tensed when he thought she might be leaving to meet that guy, the one who was considering buying her building. Would she go out with him to convince him to let her store stay right where it was?

He jerked his gaze away from the now empty doorway. He tried to tell himself it wasn't any of his concern, but he couldn't get the way she'd hurried from the room out of his mind. Something told him she wasn't rushing to meet someone, more like she had to get away. He had to remember that she wasn't Charlotte. India had already shown Ginny more caring than Charlotte ever had.

When he glanced at his mom, she was giving him one of those "Mom knows everything" looks. The problem was, she usually did. That didn't mean he was going to admit to anything yet, not when he wasn't sure if there was anything beyond their one date and that really great kiss.

To escape the questions in his mom's eyes, he moved toward where Elissa, Skyler and Verona were beginning to clean up the mess of ripped wrapping paper and used plastic cups, plates and forks. He bent over to pick up the big pink bow that had been on India's package.

"Don't worry about that," Skyler said. "We'll clean up."

"It's no problem after everything you all did to make sure Ginny's birthday was a good one."

"We love any reason for a party," Elissa said.

"Where'd India get off to?" Verona said as she scanned the room.

"I think she headed home."

He tried not to act as if he saw the meaningful look that passed between the three women, but it confirmed that something was wrong. Chances were he was the last person who should check on India, though, especially when he might very well be the reason she was upset.

After they'd cleaned the room and said their goodbyes, Liam walked over to where his parents were sitting, Ginny on his father's lap. "You about ready to go, kiddo?"

"I want to stay with Nana and Pop-Pop."

"We don't get to see her that often, so we thought we might go watch some TV, have breakfast here in the morning," his mom said as she squeezed Ginny's hand. "We can bring her out to the fairgrounds on our way out of town."

He nodded. "Okay. But you let your grandparents get some sleep tonight."

"Party pooper," his dad said.

"You can stay, too," his mom said. "It's a lovely place."

"I can't. I need to check on things tonight before I hit the hay."

After kissing Ginny good-night, he headed to his truck.

Once outside, he realized he was free to go see India. He just didn't know if that was a good idea. The woman tied him all up in knots, something he hadn't allowed to happen in a long time. Casual dating was way safer when you didn't want to get tangled up in some emotional tug of war.

But, damn, one date should have been the definition of casual. Instead, he thought about her all the time, reliving that one kiss as if it'd been the first time he'd ever kissed a woman.

With a shake of his head, he climbed into the truck and drove back toward the fairgrounds. But as he hit the mostly deserted downtown, he considered stopping at the Frothy Stein for a beer. Just as he decided he'd better just go get some sleep, he noticed a car parked farther down the street, far enough that he suspected it wasn't part of the Stein's crowd. As he drove closer, his suspicion was confirmed. India's car sat in front of her shop. Something told him she wasn't there to work.

He parked behind her and got out of the truck. As he approached the front door, he noticed one faint light shining. He saw her sitting in the front part of the store at the table where they'd shared pie that day. She didn't move, simply stared toward the main part of the store. He lifted his hand to knock, hoping he didn't scare her.

He kept his knock light, but she still jumped. He gave her an apologetic look even though she probably couldn't see it. Wondering if he just looked like a shadow, he pulled off his hat. That seemed to help her recognize him, and she slowly stood and walked toward the door. When she unlocked it, he could tell that she'd been crying. A surge of protectiveness swamped him, and it was all he could do not to take her in his arms.

"Are you okay?"

"I'm fine."

"Don't take this the wrong way, but you don't look fine."

With a sigh, India turned and walked back through the small room. Since she hadn't slammed the door in his face, he stepped inside and pushed the door closed behind him. He held his hat in his hands and didn't know if he should move any closer to her.

"I'm sorry if you're upset because of me. You said you wanted to keep things professional, and I didn't respect that."

India shook her head. "It's not that."

He chanced closing some of the distance between them, stopping at the end of the glass display case a mere couple of steps from where she stood unnecessarily straightening a dress on a mannequin.

"Then what's wrong?" he asked.

"You'll think it's crazy."

"Try me."

She glanced at him before shifting her gaze into the darkened part of the store. "Because I couldn't stand how happy your family looked together tonight."

She was right. That did sound crazy. Or maybe mean and selfish.

"It's not that I don't want you all to be happy. I'm glad that you are. It's just that watching your parents, how they are with each other, how you are with Ginny, I guess I was a little jealous. I never saw my parents like that, never experienced the kind of love you shower on Ginny from either of my parents." She laughed, but it wasn't the good kind of laugh someone uttered when they were happy. "My parents were drunks and drug addicts. I can't tell you how many times we didn't even have electricity because they didn't pay the bill. They used whatever money they managed to earn to buy drugs and alcohol."

He hated hearing this, thinking about India as a little girl going through it. But he didn't know what to do with this information. If he could go back in time and make things better for her, he would. But that wasn't possible.

"I worked my ass off to do well in school, to earn enough in scholarships so I could get out and never go back. It's part of the reason I entered that pageant, because there was scholarship money. That and the fact that for one night, I just wanted to feel pretty, like I wasn't poor little India Pike whose parents weren't worth the air they breathed."

"They were still your parents."

"In name only." She sounded so harsh, so deeply hurt by them. "You know what the real kicker was? After I went away to college, they got the wild idea to become entrepreneurs. So they started cooking meth." She shook her head in disgust. "They couldn't even do that right. Halfway through my freshman year, they blew themselves up."

"God, India."

She met his eyes. "That is what Celene Bramwell sees when she looks at me. What T.J. said to me when he was drunk that night."

"If this place has so many bad memories, why did you come back? You're smart, talented. You could have gone anywhere."

"Because despite my parents, I always loved Blue Falls. When I was a little girl, I dreamed of having a place like this store. For a long time, that's all it was, a dream. And my best friends were here. I wanted to come back and make good memories to replace the bad ones. And for the most part, I have."

"But we can't completely escape our pasts."

She shook her head.

"I'm sorry you had to go through all that, but it made you who you are, a strong woman." The words felt wrong even as he said them. Not that he wasn't sorry, because he was. But his sympathy was a throwaway line he could have as easily told someone he'd just met, not the woman who'd gotten under his skin and into his head like no one ever had. He sounded more like a shrink or a motivational speaker than someone who actually cared about her.

Because he did care about her. Something moved deep within him, something that stole his breath. Something that suddenly scared the living daylights out of him. Against his will, his feelings deepened for her in that moment. The magnitude of that change stole the air from the room, and he fought the urge to simply turn and run out the door. As he looked at India, he had no idea what to say or do. It was as if his brain had received a jolt from a cattle prod.

"You should get back to Ginny and your parents."

As he stared at her sad, tired face, he wanted to tell her that he was where he wanted to be. But common sense was telling him that this distance between them would make things easier when he left. After all, he couldn't do anything to make her past pain go away, couldn't ensure the future success of the business she'd worked so hard to build. Sometimes life just dealt you a crappy hand.

So instead of pulling her into his arms to give her some comfort, he took the coward's way out and stepped toward the door. "See you tomorrow."

"Yeah." It sounded as if it took all her energy to push out the single world.

As he left the shop and walked to his truck, he felt lower than he had in a very long time. But what good would getting even more involved with India do? Wouldn't he end up hurting her more?

Or if he were being honest, was he more concerned about getting hurt himself? He wouldn't have thought it possible. Damn it, that's why he always kept things casual. Getting serious was just too much of a minefield, for him and

Ginny. She'd already been left by her mother. He couldn't stand the idea of getting serious with someone, Ginny getting attached, and then her getting her heart broken when it didn't work out.

He slid into his truck and sat there in the dark wondering what part of his racing thoughts were the truth. Yes, he worried about Ginny getting hurt, but was he really just hiding behind his little girl?

With a sigh, he started the truck and headed toward the fairgrounds. When he pulled in, the fairgrounds looked more like an RV campground. But even with all the cowboys and stock handlers milling about, he didn't think he'd ever felt so bone-deep lonely.

INDIA DIDN'T MOVE UNTIL she saw Liam drive away down Main Street. She should really go home. Tomorrow would be long, stressful and tiring. Instead, she wandered through the dim interior of the store, letting her fingers drift through the fabrics that all looked like varying shades of gray and black in the dark. When she reached the cushy chairs outside the dressing rooms, the emotions she'd been holding in broke free.

A ragged sob escaped as she sank onto the nearest chair. She shook as tears flowed and her heart broke. How had she allowed herself to get into such a vulnerable position, one where she irrationally fell for a man who could evidently never love her back? Hadn't Liam just proved that? She'd told him about the darkest time in her life, what made her the way she was, and all he'd had to say was he was sorry. And then he'd just left.

Thinking about watching him walk out that door without a backward glance made her cry all the harder. She curled onto her side on the chair and its adjacent twin and let the sobs come. She realized all the tears weren't for Liam and what might have been. Some were the tears she'd never shed over the death of her parents, tears she'd told herself they didn't deserve. But if nothing else, Liam had been right about that—they were her parents, and some deeply buried part of the little girl she'd been loved them no matter how flawed they'd been.

As the minutes ticked by in the dark, India soaked the fabric of the chair with a lifetime of tears she hadn't even realized she'd imprisoned somewhere deep inside. She wondered if it was possible to cry so much she would simply fade away.

Chapter Thirteen

Liam figured the day of the rodeo festivities would be so busy he wouldn't have time to think about India. He'd been dead wrong. Somehow he managed to keep up with everything that needed to be done, but he still caught himself scanning the crowd for her. Not once was she looking back at him. He didn't like how that made him feel in his gut, in his heart, but he had no one to blame but himself.

Midway through the afternoon, Ginny came strolling into the barn wearing her new red hat and boots and holding a big, pink-frosted cupcake in her hand.

"Are your judging duties over?"

"Yep." She licked a dollop of frosting off her thumb.

"How was it? Did you have a good time?"

"There were so many cupcakes, I thought I might bust."

Liam laughed, and it felt foreign, as if he didn't have any right to laughter. "Who was the big winner?"

"A lady who made chocolate-orange cupcakes. They were so yummy!"

Liam gave the cupcake in her hand a glance. "Just how many cupcakes have you eaten?"

Ginny shrugged and gave him a look that said the answer was "Too many."

"That's it. You're having nothing but vegetables for dinner tonight."

Ginny pulled an "eww" face that had him laughing again. He ruffled her hair and turned when one of the bull riders had a question.

Liam expected Ginny to leave, to go check out some of the other festivities India and her friends had organized. But when he turned back around, Ginny still stood there with a concerned look on her face.

"What's wrong, honey?"

"India is really sad today."

His heart twisted at his daughter's words. "Did she say that?"

Ginny shook her head. "No. I can tell, though. I tried to give her a cupcake, but she said for me to keep it. I miss seeing her smile. She's pretty when she smiles."

Yes, she was. She was the most beautiful woman he'd ever met. In that moment, he wanted to say to hell with the rodeo and take India off somewhere private, to somehow find the right words for how he felt about her. But this rodeo was more important than most, and India had worked hard to make it and the accompanying events a success. If he could just get through the next couple of days, then he could figure out if there was a way to make things work between them. If India was even interested anymore.

INDIA MADE HER WAY THROUGH the various booths filled with arts, crafts and all manner of food that would make a cardiologist cringe. In the background, she could hear the announcer for the rodeo events calling out names and times. She bought a glass of lemonade and wandered over to the booth sponsored by the local tourism bureau, complete with piles of travel brochures highlighting Blue Falls' many offerings. Verona and Skyler were busy talking to a young couple, so India picked up one of Skyler's new brochures for the inn.

When the couple left the booth, her friends turned their attention to her.

"Where's Elissa?" she asked.

Skyler pointed toward the arena. "Over watching hot cowboys."

"Which is where I thought you would be, honey," Verona added.

India shook her head. "No, I need to make sure everything is running smoothly here."

"Everything is fine. Stop worrying, and go enjoy yourself."

She didn't think that watching the man who'd captured and tossed aside her heart ride a dangerous animal qualified as enjoying herself.

Verona took India's hand and squeezed it gently. "Honey, what happened? You've looked miserable all day today, and you disappeared without a word last night."

"I'm just tired. I think maybe I need a vacation."

If she lost the business, she'd have all the free time in the world. But then she wouldn't be able to afford a vacation. Catch-22.

"Are there any cupcakes left at Keri's booth?" Skyler asked, shifting the conversation in a different direction.

India shot her friend a silent thanks. "Yeah, a few."

Skyler exited the booth. "Verona, can you hold down the fort for a few minutes?"

"Sure, sweetie. Take your time." Verona let go of India's hand and went to talk with yet another visitor to the booth, who was asking about Vista Hills, the Teagues' guest ranch.

Skyler hooked her arm through India's as they headed toward the Mehlerhaus Bakery booth. "You've fallen for Liam, haven't you?"

If Elissa or Verona had asked, India knew she would have denied it. But Skyler was different. She had an easier way about her despite her perfectionist tendencies. And India felt like if she didn't confess to someone, she was going to crumble.

"Yes."

"But you're afraid to admit it because of how different you are."

"And the fact that he's leaving, and Fort Worth isn't exactly close. Not to mention I don't think he feels the same way."

"Are you kidding me? Have you seen the way he looks at you?"

India stopped walking, causing Skyler to stop, too.

"I'm so confused, Sky. One minute we have a very nice dinner together, and we kiss. But then I freak out and pull away. I understand why he wasn't all warm and fuzzy after that, but last night after the party he stopped by the shop. I went there after I left the party because I just couldn't face going home to an empty house." She met Skyler's eyes and saw genuine sympathy there. "I never thought I minded being alone until now."

"What happened when he stopped by?"

"I'd hit the breaking point, and everything just spilled out."

"You told him how you felt about him?"

"No, not that. I told him about Mom and Dad, about why I am the way I am. Driven, closed off."

"Afraid of getting hurt."

India nodded. "After I spilled everything, he just said he was sorry and left."

"Oh." Skyler glanced in the direction of the rodeo arena as the announcer told the crowd that the barrel racing was about to start. "Sometimes guys aren't good with feelings and heavy stuff."

"And sometimes they're looking for a way to get themselves out of an uncomfortable situation."

Skyler took a step to face India. "Hon, if he wanted to make a clean break, why would he have stopped to see you last night?"

India shrugged. "I don't know."

"I think you do."

"It doesn't matter now."

"If you care about him, it does matter. You've just got to figure out if you care enough about him to try to find a way to at least give the two of you a chance to work."

Could she do that? It felt as if choosing to make that final confession to Liam would be like throwing herself off a cliff and hoping he caught her.

"Now let's go get a cupcake," Skyler said.

As they approached Keri's booth, India spotted Liam standing halfway between the barn and the grandstand. And Gretchen Toliver was standing on her tiptoes next to him, planting a kiss on his cheek.

The pang in her chest stole her breath. She turned so she couldn't see them and somehow managed to go through with buying a lemon cupcake. After a few seconds of chatting with Keri, India touched Skyler's arm.

"I'm not feeling well. If you think things will be okay the rest of the night, I'm going to go home and get some rest."

"Are you okay?" Skyler's concern was almost India's undoing.

"Yeah, fine."

Judging by Skyler's expression, she knew India was running away. But she was kind enough not to point it out.

"Think about what I said. There are a lot of sparks between the two of you. I think it's worth giving a shot."

India couldn't bring herself to tell Skyler what she'd just seen. It was easier just to flee like she always did.

But as she was in the process of doing just that, she almost literally ran into Kevin.

"Oh, hey," she said, surprised to see him. He didn't seem like the rodeo type.

"Hello. You're leaving?"

"Yeah. Have a good time." She started to walk past him.

"I will if you'll blow this hoopla and go have dinner with me. I'm craving Mexican."

She almost declined him for the fourth time, but then wondered if that was the wisest course. She'd just acknowledged to Skyler that she was lonely. Wouldn't it make more sense to try to cultivate a relationship with a man who might actually be moving to Blue Falls? One who was easy to talk to and didn't make her feel as if she might crack inside.

"Sure. La Cantina sounds good after all this junk food."

Kevin's eyes widened before he ushered her to the parking area, probably thinking she might change her mind at any minute. She wasn't sure she wouldn't.

"I'll just meet you there," she said when they reached her car. "So I don't have to come back and get my car later."

"Okay, but don't stand me up."

She managed a smile, determined to see where this evening led. "Don't worry. I have tacos on the brain now."

Throughout dinner, India kept reminding herself that Kevin was exactly the kind of man she'd always wanted. And with him leaning very heavily toward buying the buildings from Celene, at least he'd be around and not hours away. She laughed at his jokes, answered questions when appropriate, even asked some of her own. But by the time the waitress cleared away their dishes, even Kevin knew she was only half there.

"Trouble in paradise?" he asked.

She opened her mouth to deny it, but she couldn't force the lie. "I'm sorry, Kevin. I really am." She looked down at her clasped fingers atop the table, ashamed that she'd tried to use him to forget about Liam.

"Don't worry about it. I knew my chances weren't great. I saw the way you looked at that cowboy at the inn."

"Evidently I'm not very good at hiding my feelings."

"Does he know?"

She shook her head.

"Then tell him. Guys are, well, we're pretty dense about these kinds of things. Take it from someone who knows."

A hint of something that wasn't teasing drew her gaze up to his.

"Believe me when I say that you shouldn't let a chance at love pass you by. I did, and she ended up marrying my best friend."

"Oh, Kevin, I'm sorry. I had no idea."

"Of course, you didn't. How could you? I try not to wear it on my sleeve. After all, what's done is done, and all we can do is move forward."

For some reason, those words from a virtual stranger sank in more than anything her friends had said since Liam Parrish strode on those long legs through her front door.

"Thank you," she said.

India hurried back to the fairgrounds and arrived just in time to see the beginning of the bronc riding competition. She'd heard from Ginny that Liam had decided to ride, so she walked to the area next to the grandstand to watch.

As she watched the first rider out, she was amazed how anyone could stay on an animal that was trying so hard to send them flying through the air. After only what seemed like three or four seconds, the horse finally won the battle and bucked the cowboy off into the dirt. She gasped, afraid he was hurt, but the guy jumped up as if nothing out of the ordinary had just happened. She guessed it hadn't.

"India."

She turned at the sound of someone calling her name and saw Elissa waving from her seat at the end of the bleachers. Skyler, Verona, Lara and Pete were seated around her. India hurried past several people sitting in lawn chairs so she wouldn't obstruct their view of the next rider and slid onto the end of the bleachers next to Skyler.

"Skyler said you went home," Elissa said.

"I changed my mind."

She caught the smile on Skyler's face but appreciated her not commenting on her unexpected return because, honestly, India had no idea what she was going to do. For now, at least, she could just sit here and watch the action.

After two more riders, the public address announcer said, "Next up we've got the man who put this rodeo together for you good folks tonight. Liam Parrish will be riding Skeeter."

India tensed as she watched Liam get set in the chute. She sent up a silent prayer that he would be safe. And just like that, the gate to the chute opened and the horse took off, bucking wildly.

"Hang on," she said. "Hang on."

The moment his eight seconds elapsed, Liam made a quick maneuver off the horse and landed in the dirt.

India was about to sigh in relief when Skeeter bucked sideways, kicking Liam so hard it knocked him over. She gasped and started to stand. Other cowboys rushed out from the edges of the arena, a couple ushering the still-bucking horse away from Liam and two more helping him to his feet. India couldn't take a breath as she watched everything happen in what felt like a horrible slow motion.

But in the next moment, Liam was walking under his own power, hobbling toward the end of the arena. When the crowd started to cheer, he took off his hat and waved it in the air.

India sank back down, her heart thudding fast, as if it were trying to catch up after missing a few beats.

Verona leaned down from the bleacher behind India. "Go to him, honey. See if he's okay."

India shook her head. "There are paramedics down there for that."

"I don't think the paramedics are the ones falling in love with that cowboy."

Her instinct was to stay where she was, but then she remembered Verona's words about growing old alone, Kevin's about grabbing opportunities for love. She also remembered that kiss Gretchen had given him and determined it would be the last. Before she lost her nerve, she stood and jumped off the bleachers to the ground.

She heard words of encouragement from her friends behind her, but she didn't turn around to acknowledge them. Instead, she scanned the end of the arena for Liam as she walked that way. When she spotted him, she started to run.

DAMN, THAT KICK WAS GOING to leave a whale of a bruise. At least he'd had a good ride before Skeeter decided to make his displeasure known.

"Hell of a ride," one of the other guys said.

"Thanks," Liam said as he leaned against a gate.

The guy looked past Liam. "This one yours?"

Confused, Liam turned to see India running toward him. His heart leaped at the sight of her.

She skidded to a halt just a couple of feet away. "Are you okay?"

Liam saw something new in her eyes, something that hadn't been there the night before, not even the night that they'd kissed. It was something deeper, more open, and it gave him a sudden surge of hope.

"I'm fine. I'll have a nice bruise, but it won't be the first time."

"Oh, okay." She sounded nervous. "Well, I'm glad you're not hurt worse."

When she started to step away, Liam reached out and grasped her hand to stop her. He didn't want her running away again.

"Go to the dance with me." He remembered what she'd felt like in his arms the last time they'd danced, and right now he wanted nothing more than to feel her close to him like that again. And the post-rodeo dance at the music hall was the perfect opportunity.

"You just got kicked by a horse."

"I am perfectly able to dance, among other things."

He couldn't tell in the dim light, but he was pretty sure she blushed. He fought hard against leading her back to the RV and making love to her. Instead, he pulled her close and captured her mouth with his.

The feel of her soft lips, the curves of her body, pushed everything else away. It took several moments for the sound of hoots from the nearby cowboys to register. India noticed the claps of approval about the same time and hid her face against his chest in embarrassment.

Liam laughed and kissed the top of her head.

India stepped back. "See you at the dance."

This time when she ran away, he didn't mind. In fact, he hadn't felt this good in ages, maybe ever.

Somehow he made it through the rest of the rodeo and all the administrative work that came afterward. While overseeing the handing out of prize money, he collected his own for second place in the bronc riding. Maybe he'd use it to take India out to a nice dinner again.

Finally, he was able to grab a quick shower, throw on clean clothes and head to the music hall. He was thankful that Jake had already taken Ginny with him and Mia. When he walked into the crowded building, he spotted the girls at the bar eating ice cream. He searched the sea of faces around him until he found India standing halfway across the room to his left talking to Skyler and Verona. No doubt Elissa was already kicking up her heels on the dance floor.

He wove his way through the crush of people until he reached her. She noticed him just as he reached out and took her hand.

"Excuse me, ladies, but I'm going to have to steal India."

This time he did see her blush right before he led her toward the dance floor. As he swirled her into his arms, he noticed she'd changed clothes, too. Gone were the shorts and top she'd had on earlier. In their places was a multi-colored minidress that had a long sleeve on one side and none on the other. It made him think of Woodstock. On her feet were her ever-present heels, this time a chunky purple pair he had no doubt she'd spent a lot of time color-coordinating with the dress. All he could think about as he held her close was ripping all of it off and leaving it in a heap in the floor of his RV.

He leaned close to her ear. "You look beautiful tonight. You always do."

"I doubt I looked beautiful last night."

He pulled back to look her in the face. "Even then. Listen, I'm sorry I was such a jerk."

"You weren't."

"I was. And I don't have an excuse. I just didn't know what to say. I didn't even know if you wanted me there. I don't have a great track record of reading women correctly."

"I didn't even know what I wanted. I felt a little Jekyll and Hyde last night."

"But tonight is different?"

She looked up at him then with those stunning blue-gray eyes of hers. "Yes. Tonight I decided to take a chance."

He caressed her cheek as they moved in time to a slow song. "What changed your mind?"

She smiled a little. "I went out to dinner with another man."

Liam halted and stared at her as everyone continued to dance around them. "Wasn't expecting that as an answer."

India nudged him back into the dance. "Kevin had asked me out several times, and I finally relented earlier. I thought maybe I was getting all tied in knots just because I was lonely."

Liam's jaw tightened. "And any guy would do?"

"I considered that might be the case, but it wasn't. He's a nice guy, and we had a good time. But even he could tell that I didn't truly want to be there."

Liam recognized a flicker of selfish hope in his chest. "Where did you want to be?"

"Where do you think?"

"Tell me."

"With you."

Liam pulled India closer still and lowered his mouth to hers. The moment their lips touched, he realized he didn't ever want to let her go.

Chapter Fourteen

India would swear her feet were floating several inches off the ground as Liam ended the kiss and met her gaze. Dancing in his arms, feeling the play of his muscles beneath her palms, was so intoxicating that she wondered why she'd waited so long to give in to her attraction to him.

That wasn't true. She did know. Fear, pure and simple. Fear of being hurt. Fear of losing focus on keeping her business afloat. Fear of people thinking she was just like her parents, which wasn't fair to Liam. He was nothing like Bob and Deena Pike, nothing. And yet somewhere along the line, she'd convinced herself that she had to end up with a certain type of man or everyone would think she'd not risen enough from her impoverished beginning. That she was okay with settling.

She'd been such an elitist fool, and shame washed over her.

She let her head rest against Liam's chest and listened to his heartbeat. She found herself moving in rhythm to it instead of the music, and he let her. With his arms around her, she'd never felt so loved even though he'd not indicated his feelings for her went that deep. All those images of well-dressed, world-traveling, cultured men faded from her memory like dissipating fog. In their place, she saw the various sides of Liam Parrish. The dedicated father kissing his daughter on the forehead, the dressed-up version taking her to a nice restaurant as a surprise and the sexy cowboy who rode crazy, bucking horses and took kicks from those animals as if they were minor annoyances. She found herself wondering about yet another side of Liam, what he looked like under those cowboy duds and how magnificent he'd probably be in bed.

Heat flushed her body, and she stepped back from him. "I need a break. I think my throbbing feet are revolting against me."

Really, she just needed a few minutes alone, to catch her breath, to think about how she wanted this night to end. Truth be known, she would dance in his arms until she couldn't even feel her feet anymore.

Liam rubbed his thumb across her cheek. "I'll go check on Ginny. Don't run off. I'll just have to chase you this time."

His words made her go tingly all over. She didn't think there was one square inch of her that didn't want the feel of his lips and hands on her.

She smiled then hurried toward the ladies' room. Once inside, she'd taken approximately two breaths before Elissa and Skyler came hurrying in like they had at many a high school dance, coming to squeal over how some boy had asked them to dance. India had never been the one asked, but she hadn't begrudged her friends. Not when they'd always been there for her, more like family than her own parents.

This time the smiles they were wearing were for her, and she couldn't imagine something feeling more surreal, as if she'd suddenly inhabited someone else's body.

Elissa leaned her butt against the sink next to the one in front of India. "I swear, if you don't take that man to bed tonight, I'm scheduling an evaluation of your sanity."

"Elissa," India said, then scanned the bathroom stalls behind her.

"There's no one in here. Not that it would matter. Anyone in the building can see where you two are heading."

India looked at herself in the mirror, but she didn't see any big blinking sign that said, "I'm on the verge of pulling Liam Parrish out back and having my wicked way with him."

"We're just dancing," she said.

"And kissing," Elissa added.

"And falling in love." Skyler sounded less like she was teasing and more as though her assessment of the situation made her deeply happy.

India looked over at Skyler and smiled.

"Or falling into bed," Elissa said.

India pushed at Elissa's shoulder. "You are impossible."

Elissa pulled out one of her wide smiles. "Yeah, but you love me. And I'm right. Admit it, you've been thinking about getting that man naked."

India turned toward the sink and braced herself on the edges. "All right, I admit it. It's almost the only thing I've been able to think about since he walked in here tonight. I think I might be crazy to even contemplate it."

"Nothing wrong with a little crazy."

"I know this doesn't sound like me, but I think Elissa's right," Skyler said.

India lifted her head to stare at herself in the mirror. She made the decision, then and there, that she was going to finally see what was on the other side of the walls she'd built around herself. She pushed away from the sink and turned toward her friends.

"I do, too."

Elissa clapped her hands together in victory just as a couple more women walked into the restroom. Probably thinking that India might change her mind, Elissa pushed her toward the door.

They were almost to the exit when reality slammed into India. She turned back toward her friends. "We can't. He's got Ginny."

"I think we can entertain one little girl for the night," Elissa said.

"I'm thinking a slumber party at the inn might do the trick," Skyler said. "I'll say it's for Mia before she has to start her treatments this week. We'll get Lara, Verona, anyone else we can scrounge up."

"Won't it look funny if I'm not there?" India asked.

"We'll just say you're working," Elissa said. "Workaholic that you are, no one will blink an eye."

India stuck her tongue out at Elissa.

"Save that for the tall, sexy cowboy."

As India rolled her eyes, she allowed Elissa and Skyler to spin her toward the door again. Before she could say anything else, they pushed her out.

She spotted Liam instantly, as if he were the only person in the room. Before she lost her nerve, she headed straight for him, weaving her way among the crowd without ever taking her eyes off him.

Liam saw her when she was a few feet away. Still, she didn't avert her eyes, holding his gaze and trying to tell him without words what she was thinking. A moment before she reached him and took his hand, recognition flickered in his eyes.

Without verbal explanation, she led him toward the front door and out into the night. When the noise of the music hall dimmed behind the closed door, Liam pulled her to a stop.

"I can't leave without Ginny."

She turned toward Liam. "Ginny has other plans tonight. All night."

It took a moment for what she was saying to sink in. When understanding hit, a slow smile started forming on Liam's face. Then, just as slowly, he pulled her close to him.

"Will Ginny be spending the night with you?" he asked.

"No."

He lifted a brow. "Will I?"

India licked her lips as she looked up into his eyes. "If you want to."

Liam pulled her even closer, molding his body to hers. "Oh, I want to," he said against her lips just before he captured her mouth with his. And this time, it wasn't the type of kiss they'd shared on the dance floor. It was hot, deep and wet, filled with the sounds of longing coming from both of them.

"I better get you back to my bed before I lose my control right here in this parking lot."

India had the craziest image of Liam taking her in the cab of his truck, an image that stole her breath and made her throb all over. To keep herself from dragging him there and having sex where anyone might see them, she ran her hand up his chest and pushed gently away.

"I was thinking more like my bed."

Liam's nostrils flared. "Why are we not there right now?"

His words made her heart beat faster. She broke contact as she started walking backward toward her car. "See you there."

Her heart beat like hummingbird wings all the way to her house. Liam must have been as anxious as her because he pulled in right behind her car a mere second after she parked. When she stepped out, he grabbed her around the waist and lifted her off her feet. He walked with her suspended all the way to the front door. Then he captured her mouth with his and pressed her back against the door. His hand slid down to her waist then he pulled her firmly against him, making it obvious just how ready he was for what they were about to do if they ever got inside to her bed.

"You're going to have to let me unlock the door," she breathed against his lips in between kisses.

"Am I?"

The man was driving her mad with longing. She'd never felt this way, and if she didn't do something to sate this hunger soon she felt as if her body was going to combust.

"As interesting as it might be, I don't think I want to give my neighbors quite that type of show."

Liam kissed his way along her jawline. "I'd make it more than interesting," he whispered against her ear.

Her head spun with the possibilities, but she somehow found the strength to push him far enough away so that she could retrieve her key and unlock the door.

But once they were inside with the door closed and locked behind them, Liam simply stood there looking at her. Had she broken the moment and given him too much time to think? In the space of a few steps, could he have had second thoughts?

"Is something wrong?" she asked.

"No." He stared at her a couple more seconds. "Are you sure, India?"

"Yes." She didn't hesitate because she *was* sure. In the back of her mind she knew he was leaving tomorrow, that she might never see him again. She tried not to think about how she'd feel when he drove away, but for tonight she wanted to be with him in every way possible. "I'm absolutely sure."

In three excruciatingly slow strides, he was flush against her. "Then I hope you don't have any plans for the next few hours." He bent and scooped her off her feet, much like he had that first day they'd met.

If she were honest with herself, she'd started falling for him that day, when he'd shown the first sign of what she'd really always wanted in a man—one who put others before himself.

He found his way to her bedroom as if he'd been there before and went straight to her bed. He laid her down across it and followed her. When he stretched his long body along hers, a powerful heat flushed all through her like a flash fire. His mouth captured hers again, and she tossed his hat somewhere across the room before running her fingers through his hair, pressing him closer.

Liam's arm circled around her and pulled her close as his mouth started a journey from her lips to her neck and down between her breasts. He pushed the fabric aside and kissed the swell of her right breast, then the left. When his tongue darted out and followed along the path his lips had taken, she rose up against him, wanting more.

"Too much clothing in the way," he breathed.

"I agree." Even the sound of her own voice, breathless, needy, made her want him more. With fumbling fingers, she started unbuttoning his shirt. When it was open to his waist, her mouth watered and she couldn't help but run her fingertips along all that toned, smooth flesh. Before she could talk herself out of it, she lifted her head and kissed him there like he had her.

It evidently pushed a new button in Liam because the next thing she knew he'd urged her back against the bed and was making quick work of undressing her. She helped where she could with her own clothes then helped him free first his belt, then the button at the top of his fly, then his zipper.

Her body vibrating at some new frequency, she slid her

hands into the top of his jeans and pressed his hips against hers. The throbbing in the lower half of her body grew in intensity, demanding to be satisfied.

"I'm going to make love to you, India."

"Good."

With a chuckle, Liam slid off the rest of his clothes then lifted her so she was lying the right way on the bed instead of crossways. When he slid alongside her, she captured his mouth, taking the initiative. Words of love were on her lips, but something held her back from saying them, maybe fear that if she spoke them he would stop and she'd never know what it felt like to have him inside her.

Liam rolled on top of her and took a moment to stare at her face, to gently push her loose hair back. Then as he held her gaze, he parted her legs and slid slowly inside her.

Of their own accord, India's eyes closed and she pressed her head back into her pillow. She gasped when Liam slid all the way in, filling her like she couldn't have ever imagined. Even so, she wanted more. Instinct had her pushing upward, prompting him to move.

Liam moaned, a sound that set her desire ablaze. He pulled almost all the way out before plunging back in. With each stroke, he moved the tiniest bit faster than the time before, driving her mad. She couldn't decide if she wanted him to speed up or continue the beautiful agony of slowly building to completion.

India ran her hands up and down his back, loving the play of his muscles, ones he used to stay astride powerful animals.

When she opened her eyes, she saw him watching her.

"My God, you're beautiful," he said. "I love watching how you react to me."

His words and the sight of him moving above her threw even more fuel onto the fire. India slid her hands slowly down his back until she reached his hips. She dug her fingers into that flesh, urging Liam to increase the pace. He complied, causing her to breathe in ragged gasps. Her body flooded with heat, a delicious tingling, and in that moment when they found their almost simultaneous release, a love so pure and real filled her that she hung on to Liam for fear it was all a fantasy.

Liam collapsed against her, shifting his weight so she wouldn't be crushed by his bigger body. He pulled her close and wrapped his arm around her, guiding her head to lie on his shoulder.

"Are you okay?" he asked, his breath wafting across the top of her head.

She flattened her palm against his chest and smiled at the warmth of that taut flesh. She'd caused that heat. "Yes. Are you?"

He laughed a little. "At the moment, I'm the king of okay."

They lay there in silence, and India couldn't remember ever feeling so happy. The fact that Liam was leaving in the morning tried to spoil everything, but she pushed it away. All she wanted was to live in the moment. Well, that wasn't all she wanted. As she shifted her body onto Liam's and trailed her lips from his chest to his neck and eventually his mouth, she felt him harden against her thigh.

They made love again, slow and sweet and beautiful. As their bodies cooled afterward, Liam grabbed a thin quilt and draped it over them both.

"You're incredible," Liam said, his voice already sounding drowsy.

She smiled as she lay her cheek against his chest. "So are you."

And I love you.

INDIA STOOD AT THE END OF Main Street as the sun rose. In the distance, she saw Liam walking away from her, heading north. She reached out to him and called his name. He wasn't so far that he couldn't hear her, but he didn't turn, didn't acknowledge her in any way. She screamed louder, but it only seemed to make him move faster. He grew smaller by the moment, prompting her to cry out louder still.

She tried to run after him, but her feet wouldn't move. "Liam!" She mouthed his name, but this time nothing came out. She tried again, but her voice was gone.

Cruel laughter from behind her drew her attention. Even though she knew it was a mistake, she turned to look. Celene Bramwell laughed at India's futile effort to keep Liam at her side.

"Stop laughing." This time, the words came.

"But it's funny," Celene said. "You actually thought someone cared about you enough to stay. When has that ever happened?"

"Skyler and Elissa."

India blinked, and Celene turned into her mother. She wore a pitying look on her haggard face. "They didn't stay for you. You just happened to be where they stayed."

"No." India choked on the word. When she blinked, her mother had turned into her father. He wore a sneer of contempt.

"There you are, thinking you're good enough to have a man love you. What is there to love in you? You're self-centered, a snob, not half as good as you think you are. If you cared for him, you'd stay out of his life, let him find someone he can love back and not just pity."

India shook her head as tears spilled over. "No, that's not true. Liam cares about me."

But when she jerked her gaze back in the other direction,

Liam was gone. Behind her, her father's laugh was joined by her mother's, Celene's, then more until it felt as if the entire population of Blue Falls was laughing.

India jerked awake feeling as if she were about to cry. It took a few seconds for the dream to fade enough for her to realize that Liam hadn't run away. He was there in her bed beside her, deep in sleep. She smiled and almost touched him. But something stopped her. Maybe it was the dream, or maybe it was just common sense returning with the dawn. Today he was leaving, and the likelihood of this ever happening between them again wasn't very good. Even if they had the best of intentions, eventually it would prove too hard unless one of them was willing to uproot their entire life on the chance that things would work out.

As she watched the rise and fall of his chest, she realized that Liam might not feel about her the way she did about him. It was different for guys. Caring enough to have sex with a woman wasn't the same thing as loving her.

She swallowed hard against the lump invading her throat and batted away tears. She refused to regret this, not when it had made her feel more alive than she ever had. For those few hours in his arms, she'd been free. And she would have loved him for that if for nothing else. She loved him enough to not ask him to change for her. Besides, he wouldn't be the only one affected. He had a child to think of, and jerking Ginny away from everything she knew just so he could be with a woman he barely knew, who he'd spent the night with one time, wasn't fair. Ginny had everything India had dreamed of as a child, and she refused to ruin that.

She wanted to kiss Liam one last time so much it hurt. Before she gave in to that desire, she slid from the bed and headed for the bathroom. She showered and dressed, rehearsing what she would say to Liam when she left the bathroom. She had enjoyed herself, and maybe they could get together the next time she was in the Dallas–Fort Worth area.

Only they wouldn't. Once he got back to his normal life, she wouldn't pop in one day and upset it again.

She ended up not needing any words when she returned to the bedroom. As she watched Liam sleeping, she wondered when was the last time he'd slept so deeply. She wondered for a moment if he'd felt the same the night before, free from responsibility and expectation. She wondered if there was any way they could make this work.

India wiped away a tear and shook her head. She couldn't let the need she'd had her entire life, the need to be loved, make her into a clingy woman, hanging on to a man who didn't have the same type of feelings for her.

She had to get away, to clear her head, to steel herself against the pain Liam's leaving would cause. As quietly as she could, she grabbed her purse and left the house. With Liam's truck parked behind her car, she was left with no choice but to walk to work. Luckily, she'd chosen comfortable shoes and it was still early enough that the air was still pleasant.

The entire way to the shop, she imagined Liam racing up behind her, begging her not to walk away, telling her he loved her with all his heart and they would find a way to be together. But none of that happened. As she slid the key in the front door of the shop, she felt as if the moment she stepped across that threshold the magic of the night before would disappear. She paused and looked down the street, but instead of Liam all she saw was a truck pulling a horse trailer, one of the rodeo riders getting an early start back home or on to the next rodeo.

Her heart heavy, she stepped into the quiet of the shop. But even the familiarity of all she'd built didn't offer her comfort this morning. She sank onto the stool behind the cash register and stared out the window. It wasn't until she noticed a sign in the bakery window that she realized she hadn't even left Liam a note.

Maybe that was a good thing. Perhaps a clean break would be easier, with no awkward words or fumbled apologies. She wondered if she'd ever see him again.

She bit her lip when it trembled. She would most definitely see him again. Even if he never again crossed her path, Liam Parrish was sure to inhabit her dreams for a very long time to come.

LIAM ROLLED OVER, STILL half-asleep and drugged with that morning-after-great-sex feeling. He reached for India but found the other half of the bed empty. He blinked against the morning light then rolled over to look toward the bathroom. But the door stood open to reveal it was as empty of India as the bedroom. He smiled when he thought she might be making him breakfast.

Laughing at how he might shock her if he strolled into the kitchen naked, that's exactly what he did. His smile died when he found it also empty. He turned and scanned the living area.

"India?"

He knew instantly that she was gone. His heart sank as he was yanked back nine years, to the morning after he'd taken Charlotte to bed. He wandered through the entire house, looking for a note that wasn't there. Cold settled in his stomach. He'd thought she was different, but had he been duped again? Had her sudden turnaround the night before simply been her satisfying her curiosity because she knew she wouldn't have to deal with him after today?

After several seconds of staring at the bed they'd shared, he didn't even take the time to shower. He dressed as quickly as he could and headed for the front door, not wanting to be there a moment longer. He didn't even care how much noise he made as he slammed his truck door and squealed away from her house. Let her explain to her neighbors why an angry man was leaving her house early in the morning.

By the time he reached his RV, he wasn't any less angry. But he'd decided that she would never know it. If he saw her again, he'd act as if nothing had happened—because no matter what words he'd been on the verge of saying the night before, evidently nothing of any importance had happened. At least not to India. But him? No matter what kind of facade he wore, his heart had taken a punch harder than the horse's kick the night before. And it was going to take a lot longer to heal than that bruise on his leg.

Chapter Fifteen

The first customers of the day weren't customers at all. When India walked out of the main display room where she'd been needlessly straightening shelves of purses, she stopped in her tracks. Elissa, Skyler, Verona and Ginny stood in the front room, all with differing levels of expectation on their faces.

"What are you all doing here?" She tried to hide the panic in her voice, but she wasn't entirely successful judging by the shift in her friends' expressions.

"Because this is where I texted Liam to pick up Ginny," Skyler said, looking like a kid who'd been caught in a mistake.

India tried to relax her rigid stance and walked behind the jewelry counter. "What time is he coming by?"

"I'm not sure. Should I call him and make other plans?"

India hesitated answering, a part of her wanting very much to see Liam again.

Ginny rested her hands on the corner of the jewelry case and looked up at India. "Are you going to be my mom now?"

India's mouth fell open, and she looked away from the look in the child's eyes. She couldn't take it if she identified that look as hope. "No, sweetie. Your dad and I are just friends."

"Oh."

The disappointment in that single word broke India's heart, and it must have showed on her face because her friends looked as if they wanted to give her a group hug and ask a million questions at the same time.

They didn't have the chance to do either because Liam walked in the front door.

He looked so good that India almost caved and begged him to forgive her for walking out that morning without a word. But with Ginny's words still ringing in her ears, she knew she couldn't. His and Ginny's lives were back in Fort Worth. Hers, at least for now, was here.

When Liam barely looked at her, she did her best not to let her hurt show. Maybe she'd done the right thing. Maybe he'd just been caught up in the moment, a guy looking to get laid. That didn't ring true with her, but it wasn't as if she was an expert on men.

It suddenly occurred to her that she was no better than Charlotte, leaving while he slept as if she'd never been there at all. India opened her mouth to apologize, but Liam spoke first, cutting her off.

"Let's go, Ginny. Time to go home."

For a moment, Ginny had a look of mutiny on her face. But then she simply ran around the jewelry case and hugged India.

It took all of India's willpower not to cry as she hugged Ginny back. With a final squeeze, she gently pushed the girl away. "Go on, now. You've got a long drive ahead of you."

"I'll miss you," Ginny said.

Good Lord, the girl was killing her. "I'll miss you, too, sweetie."

India made the mistake of glancing toward her friends.

Elissa especially wore a look that begged her to stop this, to explain what was going on.

For a moment, India's gaze met Liam's. She desperately searched for something there that would change her mind about letting him go, but there was nothing. It was as if he was already gone. "Goodbye, Liam."

All he did was nod before he led Ginny out the door.

India refocused her attention on a pair of pearl earrings in the glass case in front of her. She couldn't watch Liam and Ginny drive away.

Elissa stepped up to the other side of the case. "What are you doing? Go stop him."

"I can't."

"You can. You love him. I can see it written all over your face. We all can."

India forced herself to meet Elissa's eyes. "That's why I have to let him go."

"That's the dumbest bunch of self-sacrificing malarkey I've ever heard."

"How do you envision this playing out, Elissa? One of two things has to happen. Either I give up my business, my life here in Blue Falls and move to Fort Worth on the off chance it works out between Liam and me. Or I pull a really selfish move and ask him to uproot not only himself but his daughter from everything she's ever known."

"She obviously cares about you," Verona said, though she wasn't as adamant as she'd once been.

"Missing me is one thing, and that will fade because she hasn't known me that long. Asking her to leave her friends, her school, her home—that's another entirely."

Skyler stayed quiet. When India looked at her, she could tell her friend knew she was right.

But if she was right, why did it feel like her heart was going to crumble to dust?

LIAM LOOKED OVER when he heard Ginny sniffle, and it made him angry at India all over again.

"How about we go out for ice cream when we get home?" he asked, wanting to take his daughter's pain away. How he wished an ice cream sundae would cure his own heartache.

"I don't want any ice cream," Ginny said. She continued to stare out the window on her side of the truck.

"You knew we had to go home, honey. This is the way it always is when we do a rodeo."

"But I wanted to stay."

So had he, but that wasn't really practical, was it? Still, he couldn't help how his mind kept wandering back to Blue Falls and India as he drove farther away. Against his better judgment, he kept trying to think of reasons to go back. Because when their eyes had met just before he'd guided Ginny out of the front door of Yesterwear, he'd seen something in India's, something he'd never seen in Charlotte's. And India had obviously cared about Ginny, which also made her totally different than Charlotte.

Then why had he left? Why hadn't he fought for her?

Because maybe India was right to handle things the way she had. How realistic was it that they could make a long-distance relationship work long-term?

He squeezed the steering wheel, wishing he could shrink the distance between Blue Falls and Fort Worth. As the miles ticked by and Ginny stayed quiet, he let his mind wander. He began to fantasize that absence would make India's heart grow fonder. Because his heart was about as fond of India Pike as a heart could get. But the next move had to be hers, not because he was stubborn but because he knew that anything between them would never work until India was finally able to overcome her fears for good.

He tried not to think about how that might never happen.

INDIA KEPT TELLING HERSELF that every day her heart would hurt a little less, but by the end of the first week after Liam had left Blue Falls she acknowledged she was lying to herself. Though she knew it was a mistake, she drove by the fairgrounds. Seeing them empty only made her feel worse, so she immediately turned around and headed to work.

When she reached downtown, however, there was still an hour before she had to open. She crossed the street to the bakery and walked inside. Thankfully, Keri wasn't working, so India didn't have to face the look of pity on her friend's face.

"Good morning," said Josephina, Keri's sister-in-law, who'd just married Keri's brother Carter a couple of months before.

"Good morning."

"What can I get for you?"

"Bear claw and a large coffee."

Once India had her breakfast and handed over payment, she said goodbye and headed out the door. Only she didn't cross the street. For the first time since she'd opened Yesterwear, it didn't offer her any comfort. Instead, she started walking down the sidewalk, saying hello to a few of the other shop owners as she passed them.

When she reached the edge of downtown, she stopped. In the distance, she saw Verona on her regular morning walk on the path that circled the lake. Suddenly, a sight India had seen dozens of times seemed so incredibly lonely. Verona was a good woman, caring, funny, and yet she was alone. And India didn't even know why. Had she passed up a chance at love? Did she regret it? Or had she never gotten the chance to grab true love for her own?

Before Verona could see her, India turned around and walked back toward the heart of downtown. Once she reached the nearest end of the shopping district, she waited to cross the street. She spotted Jake and Mia heading out of town, probably on their way to Austin for Mia's second cancer treatment. They both waved. Even in the face of chemo, Mia had a smile for her. As they passed by, India watched them, her heart going out to Jake. He had to be scared to death, and he was facing this alone.

By the time India reached the front door of her shop, it felt as if the universe was trying to tell her something. She tried to argue with it, using the same reasons she'd given her friends, but the universe didn't give up as easily.

She sank onto one of the chairs at the table in the front room and stared at the carved daisies around the edges of the table, tracing them with her fingertip. She had no idea how much time had passed when she finally accepted that she had to tell Liam how she felt, every last bit of it. If she didn't, she knew she'd never have any peace.

She also knew that she didn't have the courage to tell him face-to-face or even on the phone. It might make her a coward, but the depth of what she felt for him made it impossible for her to lay out all her feelings and then have him tell her to her face that he didn't feel the same way. At least if she wrote down how she felt and he rejected her, she could mourn in private.

It took several minutes for her nerves to calm down enough for her to write legibly. But with a deep breath, she finally put pen to paper. It took several pages because she held nothing back, and the moment she finished she stuffed the letter into an envelope, addressed it and walked it down to the mailbox on the corner. If she put it in her outgoing mail, she knew she might very well rip it up before the mail carrier picked it up.

The moment the letter left her fingers and fell into the

dark belly of the mailbox, she felt as if she'd just thrown a pair of dice that would decide the course for the rest of her life.

LIAM COULDN'T STOP HIS GAZE from drifting to the letter sitting on the edge of his desk, just like it had since it had been delivered the day before. The dang thing even smelled like her, the hint of roses refusing to leave him alone.

He tried focusing on work, but it was no use. He had to know what was in that envelope. When he ripped it open, he saw it contained several pages of stationery. He smiled a little at that. It was so very India to use classy stationery when most of the world emailed or texted.

With a deep breath he sat back in his chair and started to read.

Dear Liam,
I hope I am doing the right thing by writing this letter. But there are things I have to say, and it's the God's honest truth that I'm too nervous to tell you in person. There is so much that I want to say, to explain about myself and why I am the way I am, but I'll just start off by saying that watching you leave that last day broke my heart.

Liam's own heart leaped at her admission. He continued reading as she started at the beginning, telling him about her childhood, how she'd gradually built walls around her heart without even realizing it. Even though she had friends, she'd never truly let herself be free to experience the full range of emotions—until the night they'd made love. He read page after page, feeling as if he were watching a movie of India's life, caring more deeply for her with each turn of a page. He knew how hard it must have been for her to bare her entire soul to him like this.

He flipped over to the final page.

Even if you've read this far, I know that it might not make a difference. I know you and Ginny have your life in Fort Worth, and part of the reason I let you go without a word was because I didn't feel I had the right to ask you to give that up. I understand spending a lot of time and effort to build something you're proud of. So if you don't feel the same and don't respond, I'll understand. But I want you to know the full truth, that sometime during your stay in Blue Falls, I fell in love with you. Honestly, I think it started that first day when you scooped me up into your arms when I broke the heel off that stupid shoe.

I'm going to send this now before I lose my nerve. If you feel the same, I'll be happier than I've been in my entire life. If you don't, don't feel guilty. I will find a way to go on, just like I always have. And I'll wish you and Ginny nothing but the best.

Love,

India

To make sure he wasn't dreaming, Liam read the entire letter over again, slower this time. When he got to her declaration of love, a smile stretched his lips. His mind raced with options for what to do next. Finally, he settled on what had to come first. He stood, carefully folded the letter and slipped it back into the envelope. Then he headed for the door. He glanced at his assistant as he stepped into the outer office.

"Connie, I'm taking the rest of the afternoon off to spend with my daughter."

INDIA WAITED FOR THE MAIL carrier to leave before she grabbed the stack of new mail and sifted through it, her heart beating fast. As she reached the last envelope and saw it was a bill from the electric company, her hope died—just as it had for the past two weeks. The same as it had every time the phone rang but it wasn't Liam calling or the front door opened and he didn't walk through it.

It was time to accept the answer he'd given her by not responding. She'd given him that option, and she had to live with it. He'd either read the letter or thrown it away unopened because it hadn't been returned to sender.

She'd told him that she'd find a way to get on with her life, but right now that felt like an insurmountable task. Still, she had to try. So she turned to the only thing she could, her work. After giving the entire shop a good cleaning and changing out the display in the front window, her heart still wasn't any lighter. If anything, it'd grown heavier. But she had to push on. If she didn't keep going, she'd never get past this horrible, consuming ache.

When she'd found out about the potential sale of the building, she'd stopped ordering stock. Still, her last order had come in the day before and needed unpacking. Hoping she'd get that high that normally came from opening up new shipments full of beautiful things, she headed for the stockroom.

Halfway through unpacking the boxes of dresses, jackets and accompanying accessories, she heard the front door open. She tossed aside the packing material surrounding her and headed for the door of the stockroom. Before she could reach it, someone appeared there, filling the space.

India gasped. A couple of seconds ticked by as she focused on the man in the doorway.

"Liam?" She blinked, hoping he wasn't a figment of her imagination, of her desperate yearning to see him again.

"In the flesh."

"What—what are you doing here?" She reached out a hand and grasped the edge of a sturdy storage shelf to steady herself.

"I'm in town on business."

"Oh." Her heart sank so fast she doubted she was able to hide her feelings. "I hadn't heard about another rodeo in the area."

"There's not, yet. But that might change."

She simply stared at him, unable to think what to say next. He looked so good, and she ached to run into his arms.

"I've been talking to some local officials about hosting three more rodeos here, maybe even moving my company headquarters to Blue Falls."

India's legs shook as hope blazed to life within her.

"It'll lower my operation costs, and I like the scenery. There's just one more thing that has to fall into place before I'll pull the trigger on the move."

India swallowed then somehow found her voice. "What's that?"

He took several slow steps into the storage room, making it feel infinitely smaller. He didn't stop until he was close enough she could touch him.

"What you said in your letter, is it still true?"

"Which part?"

"That you love me."

She resisted touching his face, afraid her hand would find nothing but air, that he would disappear like a mirage. "Yes."

He smiled. "That's good because I'm hopelessly in love with you, India Pike."

India sank down onto a box, her legs no longer able to support her.

"Are you okay?"

She looked up at Liam. "Say it again."

Liam lowered himself to one knee in front of her and framed her face with his hand. "I love you, India. Ginny loves you. And it's time you love yourself as much as we love you." He rubbed his thumb over her cheek. "We can go as slowly as you want, but I need to know I'll be making the right decision if I move here."

A tremendous happiness, bigger and fuller and brighter than anything she'd ever imagined, filled India. She smiled and nodded.

"Well, that's good. Because I just paid a substantial down payment on this building and the one next door."

"What? Why would you do that?" She knew the price tag Celene was asking.

"Because I love you, and no one is going to threaten the dream of the woman I love."

India took his face in her hands and kissed him, filling the kiss with the depth of her love.

When they finally stopped kissing, she didn't want to let him go. "So will my rent go up?"

It took him a moment to catch her meaning. She liked to think it was because he was so dazed by her kiss.

"Well, you'll be sharing the extra space with me since I'm going to put my office on the second level next door. But we'll think of a way for you to pay me."

She swatted him. "I'm not that kind of girl."

He kissed her again. "Would it make any difference if I

told you that I plan to make you my wife someday, whenever you're ready?"

Tears pooled in India's eyes, but this time there was no sadness attached to them. "The way I feel right now, I'd marry you tomorrow."

"Be careful or I might take you up on that."

"Go ahead."

Liam leaned back and took her hand in his. "I don't have a ring for you right now, but I'm going to ask you, anyway." He swallowed visibly, making her smile. "India Pike, will you be my wife and a mother to my daughter?"

"Yes, I will."

She had no idea how long they kissed after that, but she didn't care. Eventually, the sound of voices in the shop drifted back to them, and Liam helped her to her feet. Neither of them let go of the other's hand as they walked out of the storage room and toward the front of the store.

Elissa, Skyler and Verona caught sight of them as they approached.

"We came to see how you were and ask you to lunch, but I'm guessing you're just fine and have other lunch plans," Elissa said.

Liam pulled India close to his side. "As a matter of fact I'm starving," he said. "I haven't had a bite to eat all day."

"To the Primrose, then," Verona said.

"One thing first," India said. "Skyler, when's the next time your banquet room is free on a Saturday?"

"I'll have to check the schedule back at the inn. Why?"

India looked up at Liam, who nodded, then back at her friends. "Because we're going to need it for a wedding."

All three of the other women screamed at the same time, making India laugh. And then they were on her, pulling her away from Liam and smothering her with hugs. She hugged them all back but caught Liam's gaze.

"I love you," she mouthed.

"I love you more," he said back.

She doubted that was possible, but she let him think it.

* * * * *

Be sure to look for HAVING THE COWBOY'S BABY,
the next book in Trish Milburn's
Blue Falls, Texas, series.
Available in September 2013
wherever Harlequin American Romance is sold.

COMING NEXT MONTH
from Harlequin® American Romance®

AVAILABLE JUNE 4, 2013

#1453 A COWBOY'S PRIDE
Pamela Britton

An accident changes Trent's world, and Alana is determined to help him. But once he's back on his feet, will he go back to his glamorous rodeo life and leave her behind?

#1454 HIS BABY DREAM
Safe Harbor Medical
Jacqueline Diamond

Widower Peter Gladstone wants a child. He never expected his egg donor, who is supposed to remain anonymous, to become a friend...and more. How can he tell her they may have a baby on the way?

#1455 DESIGNS ON THE COWBOY
Roxann Delaney

Dylan Walker's sister has hired Glory Andrews to renovate his ranch house, and Dylan is not happy about it. The cowboy just wants to be left alone, but Glory is hard to ignore!

#1456 THE RANCHER SHE LOVED
Saddlers Prairie
Ann Roth

When former rodeo champion Clay Hollyer meets up with Sarah Tigarden, the writer who panned him in print, sparks fly—and not the good kind. At first...

You can find more information on upcoming Harlequin®
titles, free excerpts and more at www.Harlequin.com.

HARCNM0513

REQUEST YOUR FREE BOOKS!
2 FREE NOVELS PLUS 2 FREE GIFTS!

HARLEQUIN®

American ★ Romance®

LOVE, HOME & HAPPINESS

YES! Please send me 2 FREE Harlequin® American Romance® novels and my 2 FREE gifts (gifts are worth about $10). After receiving them, if I don't wish to receive any more books, I can return the shipping statement marked "cancel." If I don't cancel, I will receive 4 brand-new novels every month and be billed just $4.74 per book in the U.S. or $5.24 per book in Canada. That's a savings of at least 14% off the cover price! It's quite a bargain! Shipping and handling is just 50¢ per book in the U.S. and 75¢ per book in Canada.* I understand that accepting the 2 free books and gifts places me under no obligation to buy anything. I can always return a shipment and cancel at any time. Even if I never buy another book, the two free books and gifts are mine to keep forever.

154/354 HDN F4YN

Name	(PLEASE PRINT)	

Address		Apt. #

City	State/Prov.	Zip/Postal Code

Signature (if under 18, a parent or guardian must sign)

Mail to the Harlequin® Reader Service:
IN U.S.A.: P.O. Box 1867, Buffalo, NY 14240-1867
IN CANADA: P.O. Box 609, Fort Erie, Ontario L2A 5X3

Want to try two free books from another line?
Call 1-800-873-8635 or visit www.ReaderService.com.

* Terms and prices subject to change without notice. Prices do not include applicable taxes. Sales tax applicable in N.Y. Canadian residents will be charged applicable taxes. Offer not valid in Quebec. This offer is limited to one order per household. Not valid for current subscribers to Harlequin American Romance books. All orders subject to credit approval. Credit or debit balances in a customer's account(s) may be offset by any other outstanding balance owed by or to the customer. Please allow 4 to 6 weeks for delivery. Offer available while quantities last.

Your Privacy—The Harlequin® Reader Service is committed to protecting your privacy. Our Privacy Policy is available online at www.ReaderService.com or upon request from the Harlequin Reader Service.

We make a portion of our mailing list available to reputable third parties that offer products we believe may interest you. If you prefer that we not exchange your name with third parties, or if you wish to clarify or modify your communication preferences, please visit us at www.ReaderService.com/consumerschoice or write to us at Harlequin Reader Service Preference Service, P.O. Box 9062, Buffalo, NY 14269. Include your complete name and address.

HAR13R

SPECIAL EXCERPT FROM

 HARLEQUIN®

American ★ Romance®

A COWBOY'S PRIDE

by Pamela Britton

A wounded cowboy. His gorgeous physical therapist. What could go wrong?

"Welcome to the New Horizons Ranch," Rana Jensen said, tipping up on her toes in excitement.

No response.

Alana McClintock recognized Trent Anderson from watching him on TV. It looked as if he hadn't shaved in a few days, his jaw and chin covered by at least a week's worth of stubble.

"Good to see you, Trent," Cabe called out.

No response.

Tom hopped inside the bus and released the wheelchair. And suddenly the longtime rodeo hero was face-to-face with the small crowd who'd gathered to greet him.

"Welcome to New Horizons Ranch," Rana repeated happily.

Still no response.

The cowboy didn't so much as lift his head.

Tom pushed the wheelchair onto the lift. Sunlight illuminated Trent Anderson's form. Still the same broad shoulders and handsome face. It was his legs that looked different.

"Don't expect much of a conversation from him," said Tom.

HAREXP0613

"He hasn't spoke two words since I fetched him from the airport. Starting to think he lost his voice along with the use of his legs."

That got a reaction.

"I can still walk," Trent muttered.

Barely from what she'd heard. Partial paralysis of both legs from midthigh down. There'd been talk he'd never walk again. The fact that he had some feeling in his upper legs was a miracle.

"I'll show you to your cabin, Mr. Anderson," Rana said, coming forward.

"Don't touch me." He spun the aluminum frame around. "I can do it myself."

Alana took one look at Rana's crushed face and jumped in front of the man.

"*You* have no idea where you're going." She placed her hands on her hips and dared him to try and run her down.

"I'll find my way."

He swerved around her.

She met Cabe's gaze, then looked over at the bus driver. They both stared at her with a mix of surprise and dismay. "First cabin on the left." She stepped to the side. "Don't let the front door hit you in the butt."

Three stunned faces gazed back at her, though she didn't bother looking at Trent again. Yeah, she might have sounded harsh, but the man was a jerk.

Too bad she would have to put up with him for three weeks.

Be sure to look for A COWBOY'S PRIDE from Harlequin American Romance. Available June 4, 2013, wherever Harlequin books are sold!